PRAISE FOR

A PARTICULAR
KIND OF
BLACK MAN:

"Wild, vulnerable, lived. . . . A study of the particulate self, the self as a constellation of moving parts."
—*The New York Times Book Review*

"[A] tender, cunning debut . . . Folarin pulls off the crafty trick of simultaneously bringing scenes to sharp life and undercutting their reliability, and evokes the complexities of life as a second-generation African-American in simple, vivid prose. Folarin's debut is canny and electrifying."
—*Publishers Weekly*

"This searing, powerful novel is a stunning debut by Tope Folarin, offering a look into the disorienting life of a first-generation Nigerian-American. . . . Folarin has written a compelling, lyrical story about alienation and identity, the kind that sticks inside you long after you've finished reading."
—*Nylon*

"Tope Folarin's *A Particular Kind of Black Man* stopped me dead in my tracks and consumed my day in a helpless trance. One feels as if someone else's mirror has appeared, and the longer one stares into it, the more something reflected becomes . . . oneself. A radical act."

—Luis Alberto Urrea, author of
The House of Broken Angels

"From the breathless first sentence, to the devastating last, this is a particularly mesmerizing kind of novel."

—Marlon James, author of
A Brief History of Seven Killings

Tope Folarin's writing is smart, spry, tender, funny, and inventive, much like the unforgettable main character of *A Particular Kind of Black Man* himself. Through this narrative of one young man's childhood and adolescence, Folarin urges us to think about belonging, family, memory, and the very act of storytelling anew. An energetic, accomplished debut."

—Angela Flournoy, author of
The Turner House

"Deeply observed and abundant with strange poetry, Folarin's novel charts a terrifying and radiant journey of growing up in an identity and family that is perpetually in flux. I tore through this book as if in a fever dream . . . its uncanny reality remained with me long after it was over."

—Jenny Zhang, author of
Sour Heart

"A young man grows up distanced from family, country, and his beloved mother; so begins the attrition of his sense of self. In this emotionally evocative and immensely moving story, Tope Folarin shows how the need to belong lives first in the heart. By combining the immigrant's tale with a coming-of-age story Folarin has brought new power to both narratives. He is a writer of talent and great promise."

—Aminatta Forna, author of
The Devil That Danced on the Water
and *Ancestor Stones*

"*A Particular Kind of Black Man* is an audacious debut, a book that is many things at once: a profound immigration narrative, a moving coming of age story, and an appraisal and defense of the novel as an essential 21st-century art form. The structure—fluid, slippery, a suspended chord in search of resolution—echoes the journey of the protagonist, and, indeed, of America. In these brilliant, searing, heartbreaking, and hopeful pages, Tope Folarin has given us a novel that many of us will revisit for years to come."

—Jeffery Renard Allen, author of
the novels *Song of the Shank*
and *Rails Under My Back*

"In *A Particular Kind of Black Man*, Tope Folarin shows the deeply personal geography of migration, and the points on this map are shaped by the hopes and terrors that the mind conjures. Each stop on Tunde Akinola's journey shows him a new layer of self. He bridges the physical distance from his grandmother with calls to Nigeria, but the emotional, racial, and cultural distances in America bring a different set of challenges. Tope Folarin writes with a mosaic of perspectives, and the fluidity and insight make this a well-layered and deeply felt debut."

—Ravi Howard, author of
Driving the King

"Arresting and insightful, Folarin's *A Particular Kind of Black Man* is one of those books that refuses to let you go till the very end. Tunde's world—broken and alive, vivid, and painful—bursts from these pages with unforgettable honesty and heart. This is a story about exiles and departures, about the continual search for what has been in front of us all along. A gripping, achingly beautiful debut."

—Maaza Mengiste, author of
Beneath the Lion's Gaze

A PARTICULAR KIND OF BLACK MAN

TOPE FOLARIN

SIMON & SCHUSTER PAPERBACKS
NEW YORK   LONDON   TORONTO   SYDNEY   NEW DELHI

Simon & Schuster Paperbacks
An Imprint of Simon & Schuster, Inc.
1230 Avenue of the Americas
New York, NY 10020

First Simon & Schuster trade paperback edition August 2020

SIMON & SCHUSTER and colophon are registered trademarks of Simon & Schuster, Inc.

For information about special discounts for bulk purchases, please contact Simon & Schuster Special Sales at 1-866-506-1949 or business@simonandschuster.com.

The Simon & Schuster Speakers Bureau can bring authors to your live event. For more information or to book an event, contact the Simon & Schuster Speakers Bureau at 1-866-248-3049 or visit our website at www.simonspeakers.com.

Interior design by Carly Loman

Manufactured in the United States of America

10 9 8 7 6 5 4 3 2

Library of Congress Cataloging-in-Publication Data

Names: Folarin, Tope, 1981—author.
Title: A particular kind of black man / Tope Folarin.
Description: New York : Simon & Schuster, 2019.
Identifiers: LCCN 2019012960 | ISBN 9781501171819 (hardback)
Subjects: | BISAC: FICTION / Literary. | FICTION / Family Life. | FICTION / Coming of Age.
Classification: LCC PS3606.O4227 P37 2019 | DDC 813/.6—dc23
LC record available at https://lccn.loc.gov/2019012960.

ISBN 978-1-5011-7181-9
ISBN 978-1-5011-7183-3 (pbk)
ISBN 978-1-5011-7182-6 (ebook)

For Stephanie and Funmi

Task: to be where I am.
Even when I'm in this solemn and absurd
* role: I am still the place*
where creation works on itself.

—TOMAS TRANSTRÖMER

1987–88

She told me I could serve her in heaven.

She accompanied me to school each day. School was about a mile away, and a few hundred feet into my trek, just as my family's apartment building drifted out of view behind me, she would appear at my side.

I don't remember how she looked. Memory often summons a generic figure in her place: an elderly white woman with frizzled gray hair, slightly bent over, a smile featuring an assortment of gaps and silver linings. I do remember her touch, however—it felt cool and papery, disarmingly comfortable on the hottest days of fall. She would often pat my head as we walked together, and a penetrating silence would cancel the morning sounds around us. I felt comfortable, protected somehow, in her presence. She never walked all the way to school with me, but her parting words were always the same:

"Remember, if you are a good boy here on earth, you can serve me in heaven."

I was five years old. Her words sounded magical to me. Vast and alluring. I didn't know her, I barely knew her name, but the offer she held out to me each morning seemed far too generous to dismiss lightly. In class I would think about what servitude in heaven would be like. I imagined myself carrying buckets of water for her on streets of gold, rubbing her feet as angels sang praises in the background. I imagined that I'd have my own heavenly shack. I'd have time to do my own personal heavenly things as well.

How else would I get to heaven?

One day I told my father about her offer. We were talking about heaven, a favorite subject of his, and I mentioned that I already had a place there. "I've already found someone to serve," I said.

"What do you mean?"

Dad smiled warmly at me. I felt his love. I repeated myself:

"Daddy, I'm going to heaven."

"And how are you going to get there?"

I told him about the old lady, my heavenly shack, the streets of gold. My father stared at me a moment, grief and sadness surging briefly to the surface of his face. And then anger. He leaned forward, stared into my eyes.

"Listen to me now. The only person you will serve in heaven is God. You will serve no one else."

My father has told me many times that he settled in Utah because he didn't want to be where anyone else was. His cousins and siblings had left Nigeria for Athens, London, Rome, New York City, and Houston. My father wanted to be an American, but he also craved isolation, so he decided he would travel to a city in America he knew nothing about.

He left Nigeria in 1979 after a school in Utah, Weber State University, offered him a place in its mechanical engineering program. His bride, my mother, accompanied him. They arrived in a country that bore little resemblance to the country they expected. Dad, a devout fan of television shows like *Gunsmoke* and *Bonanza,* was disappointed when he discovered that cowboy hats were no longer in style, and he sadly stowed his first American purchase—a brown ten-gallon hat that he bought during a layover in Houston—in his suitcase, and under his bed. Mom arrived in America expecting peace and love—she had fallen for the music of the Beatles and the Beach Boys as a high school student in Lagos while listening to the records that her businessman father brought back from his trips abroad. Though she had imagined a country where love conquered all, where black people and white people lived together in peace and harmony, Mom and Dad arrived, instead, in a place where there were no other black people for miles around, a place dominated by a religion they'd never heard of before.

But this was America. And they were in love. They moved into a small apartment in Ogden, Utah, and started a family. I came first, in 1981, and my brother followed in 1983. Dad attended his classes during the day while Mom took care of us at home. Occasionally she explored the city while pushing my brother and me along in a double stroller. Soon enough we were all walking hand in hand.

At night my parents held each other close and spoke their dreams into existence. They would have more children. My father would start a business. They would become wealthy. They would send their children to the best schools. They would have many grandchildren. They would build their own version of paradise on a little slip of desert in a country that itself was a dream, a place that seemed impossible until they stepped off the plane, shielding the sun from their eyes, and saw for themselves the expanse of land that my father had idly pointed to on a fading map many years before.

As I look back now, especially with the knowledge of what will come after, the rest of my life set in unflattering relief, I realize that my first five years were the most ordinary of my childhood. We moved frequently, but I can only remember joy.

One of my favorite memories from this era: for some reason I'm chasing my brother around our apartment with a red crayon. When I catch him I pin him against the wall and color each of his teeth red as he screams. My mother shrieks when she sees him; she thinks he's bleeding because of the red wax that's shining from his teeth. She laughs when I tell her that the blood isn't real, and then we all laugh and I allow my brother to color my teeth as well. Then we color Mom's teeth—she prefers lime green.

Life flowed easily until we moved to Bountiful. We settled there because my father had found a job at an auto repair shop in neighboring Layton, and Bountiful was one of the few places close by with any affordable housing. My father couldn't find a job as a mechanical engineer anywhere in northern Utah, but he knew a bit about cars, and he figured he would work as a mechanic until something better came along.

My mother's illness began to reveal itself to us shortly after we moved into our two-bedroom apartment, a tiny place near the center of town with pale-yellow walls and bristly carpet. Mom's voice, once quiet and reassuring, grew loud and fearsome. Her hugs, once warm and comforting, became cold and rigid. She stopped cooking for us—sometimes my brother and I didn't eat until my father returned from work in the evening. She began to spend more time in her room, away from us.

One morning my brother shook me awake and told me that Dad was crying. I did not believe him. I didn't think such a thing was possible. We scrambled to the living room and saw Mom standing over Dad, her eyes boiling with rage. My father was naked. His clothes, now nothing more than torn rags, were arrayed haphazardly around the room. He was bleeding from a wound on his thigh, and his face was wreathed in a constellation of sweat and tears. My brother and I reached over to him but Mom cursed at us:

"GET THE FUCK OUT OF HERE!"

I was terrified. I looked at Dad. His bottom lip was shaking. His teeth were red. "Yes, go!" he said. "What are you waiting for? Go now!"

We ran. We hugged each other in the corner of our room. Moments later, my father began to scream.

Over the course of the next few days my brother and I witnessed this scene many times, my father cowering on the floor, my mother standing imperiously over him. He took her punishment whenever she descended into one of her moods, and afterward he would enter our room with a calm smile and tell us that Mom wasn't feeling like herself, but that everything would soon be OK. We tried our best to believe him.

Before long we realized the truth. After Dad left for work each morning my mother locked herself in their room. She rarely interacted with us, but occasionally she opened the door and asked us to come inside. She asked us to stand in the corner of the room, near the dresser. She pointed to various places in the room: her closet, Dad's desk, the empty space near her full-length mirror. She asked us if we saw it.

"See what, Mommy?"

"Don't you see that? What is wrong with you?"

My brother and I glanced at each other. Was this a game?

"Mommy, I don't see anything. Can we go now?"

"No! Not until you tell me what it is doing there. Tell me why it won't leave!"

Sometimes my brother and I lied. We made up stories about what we saw and my mother nodded sagely. Sometimes she disagreed with us and told us to look again. This could have been fun, but the wild look in my mother's eyes unsettled us.

Sometimes she told us that we had to leave before they came to get us. "Something about this place isn't right," she'd say. "Not right at all."

Then she'd pull up her covers, switch on the radio, and mutter herself to sleep.

I started school on September 7, 1987, a few weeks before I turned six. I was ecstatic because I'd spent much time watching the kids of my neighborhood trip past my bedroom window with books under their arms and bags on their backs, like they were departing for another world. I dimly sensed that at school I could become something more than a brother or son, that each day I went I would come back carrying knowledge that was mine alone.

My family walked with me to school that first day. I remember the principal extending her hand when I met her. I shyly extended mine as well, and as we shook hands she said, "We are very happy that you're here!"

It was in her eyes. The way she looked at me. Like I was something scary and unknown. That's how I knew I was different. On the playground all my classmates asked if they could touch my hair. I said OK. Then Simon rubbed my skin and ran away crying to the playground attendant.

"It won't come off!" he wailed. "Why won't it come off?"

I was too tired after school to ask my father any questions, too excited about everything I had just experienced, but the next day, after another kid rubbed my arm until it was raw, I asked my father why my hair was so kinky, and why I couldn't wash the brown off my skin. He shook his head and frowned. He began talking about the importance of pride, the meaning of self-respect, but I didn't really understand what he was saying.

As he spoke, I thought about the old lady I'd met a few hours before.

That morning, Dad had hugged me at the door of our apartment and told me that I'd have to walk to school by myself because he had to work and Mom wasn't feeling well. I said OK, but I was afraid because school seemed so far away.

As I walked to school, tentatively, nervously, she suddenly appeared, like I'd dreamed her into existence.

She told me her name was Mrs. Hansen, and she asked me what I was doing. I told her I was walking to school. She smiled.

"I've never seen a little black boy around here before," she said. "Where are you from?"

"I'm from here," I said. She laughed and placed a hand on my shoulder.

She spoke as we walked, and I enjoyed hearing her voice, the gentle rise and fall of it, because it somehow seemed familiar to me. She asked me questions about Dad and Mom and my brother. She told me that she'd always wanted to go to Africa, but she'd never had the chance.

When we were about a block from school she looked into my eyes and patted my head.

"I enjoyed speaking with you. You are a wonderful little boy." She blinked slowly and nodded. "Keep it up. Maybe one day you'll get to serve me in heaven. If you do, I promise you'll get everything you've ever wanted."

The happiness I felt as I turned and ran to school, the sheer joy, is something I've been searching for ever since.

I woke up that morning to my mother rubbing my hair. Mom was smiling down at me when I opened my eyes. She looked beautiful. She was dressed in her favorite outfit: a finely embroidered purple blouse covered by a flowing wrapper, a matching headdress hovering atop her small Afro. She asked me to wake up my brother and after hugging us she asked us to get dressed.

"Where are we going, Mommy?" I asked as I pulled on my pants.

"On an adventure!" she said, smiling widely. "Now hurry so we won't be late."

My brother and I moved quickly in the crisp darkness. We rushed into the living room when we were done, and Mom evaluated us in a single glance.

"Go get your backpacks and pack some clothes as well."

"Where are we going?"

"I told you, on an adventure!"

"What about Daddy?"

Mom turned and glanced at the wall.

"He's coming later, after work."

"How about school?" I asked. I'd only been in kindergarten for a month.

Mom gave me a half smile. "Don't worry! Just get ready."

We ran back to our bedroom and packed our bags with assorted socks, underwear, shirts and pants. After a few minutes we returned to the living room.

"All done!" we yelled in unison.

She laughed.

"You guys were quick! OK, now wait, someone is coming to pick us up."

We sat. My brother and I tried to blow smoke rings with the frosty air. Mom disappeared into her bedroom and when she returned she was dragging a rolling suitcase behind her.

A few records were tucked under her arm. She had replaced her headdress with a large brown cowboy hat. I'd never seen her so happy in my life.

Someone rapped on the door a few minutes later. Mom nodded at us.

"Go ahead!" she exclaimed. "This is part of the adventure!"

My brother and I raced to the door, but I got there first. There was a woman standing there. She had short red hair, and her freckles were so densely packed that I wondered how each one survived without space, without room to grow.

"How are you?" she asked. "You are so cute! Are you ready to go?"

Mom joined us at the door.

"Yes, we are ready. Let us go before it is too late. We have so much to do today."

We piled into the lady's car. I can't remember what kind of car it was, just that it was small and that my mother insisted I sit in the front. The freckled lady turned the ignition and revved the engine while my mother held my brother close. The lady turned to me and asked if I was cold. I shook my head, but we sat in the dark until I felt the heat on my shoes and face. Then she put the car into gear and we drove off.

We passed the local grocery store, Smith's, and I suddenly realized that we weren't going on an adventure.

"Mommy, where is this woman taking us?"

"I already told you! Now be quiet and enjoy the ride."

"Mommy, I don't believe you. Where are we going? Where's Daddy?"

Mom ignored me. The lady patted me on the head and turned on the radio. Stevie Wonder was singing something but I don't know what it was.

I don't remember what happened after I realized that we weren't actually going on an adventure. My mind skips, like a ruined compact disc, to a small room with bare walls at the YWCA in Salt Lake City.

I start the day with a tutor who showers me with praise; she brings books for me to read every day, and she tells me I'm the smartest kid she's ever known. Most of her books are about African American leaders, but I don't know what an African American is yet. They all look black to me. We read about George Washington Carver, Booker T. Washington, and Benjamin Banneker. She also tells me about Martin Luther King. I learn that he starts college when he's fifteen, that he attends a black school in Atlanta called Morehouse, and that he has a doctorate by the time he's twenty-six. Do I know what a doctorate is? I don't answer because I'm still thinking about the black school in Atlanta. Where is Atlanta? And how is such a thing possible in America? Only black people, only people like me in a school? This seems impossible, so I decide that the school, the city itself must be a relic of the past. My tutor smiles at me, her black hair shining. In her hands, the book looks brand-new, like no one's ever opened it before. She turns the page. I don't know what's real and what's fake anymore.

After my tutoring sessions I join my brother in the nursery. We play together until Joy stops by to pick us up. Joy has long blond hair and a jagged, ruined face. She is beautiful.

She takes us to the common room and my brother sits on her lap. We spend the afternoon watching TV shows like *The People's Court* and *The Judge*. Joy rubs my head constantly, and bends down to kiss my forehead during the commercials. I think she does this because she knows how much I miss my father. I haven't seen him since Mom took us away. She must know that I feel so alone without him, that I would give anything just to hear his voice.

Sometimes her friends join us. I only remember them in caricature. One is fat and one is skinny. Like a pair of mismatched twins they bounce around the room and my memory, orbiting our small impromptu family. By the time Joy walks us to our room my brother has fallen asleep in her arms, and I'm too tired to be scared of Mom.

The fear returns when we arrive at our door.

Sometimes Mom is better. I know she is taking medicine now, and although she is never happy, sometimes she remembers herself.

This memory will never leave me: My brother and I walk into our small apartment in the shelter and look for Mom. I glance at our spotless kitchen on the left, and our spare living room on the right. A dusty table sits in the middle of the room. Mom steps out of the bedroom; she is small and thin, and has large, wide-set eyes. Her nose is as small as a button. She turns on the radio, finds the oldies station, and begins to hum. Sometimes The Mamas and The Papas come on, sometimes the Rolling Stones, sometimes the Beach Boys, sometimes Simon and Garfunkel, sometimes Dylan, but always, inevitably, the Beatles. My mom smiles whenever she hears Paul singing. It doesn't seem odd to me then, a Nigerian woman with a Beatles obsession; the only thing I care about is that the Beatles bring her peace. I often wish the disembodied voices would skip everything else and just play the Beatles, only the Beatles, all evening, so Mom will feel better.

Sometimes Mom turns off the radio and asks us to sit on the floor. She tells us a story from her childhood, and although I remember a few of them there is one that she tells us most often, about a turtle and a seagull. If only I could remember the moral of the story, how it ends.

Mom stops cooking Nigerian food when we get to the shelter. She will only prepare frozen food, but my brother and I don't care. We're always happy when we see her busying herself in our tiny kitchen, opening the box of frozen fried chicken, the delicious rip of aluminum foil, placing the foil and chicken into the oven. Soon the savory fumes tunnel into our nostrils. She dumps a dollop of store-bought crab salad onto our plates, sometimes some fried rice from the local Chinese restaurant if she has extra money, and the fried chicken. If it's summer, the window is open, the breeze warming our backs.

To my mother, silence is love.

So we, in turn, learn to love silence. If our mother looks away as we walk in the door she is signaling her unending devotion to us. If she ignores us when we ask her a question she's actually telling us that we're smart enough to figure things out ourselves. If we call for her and she refuses to respond, we know she is hugging us all the same.

To my mother, awareness is anger.

If we feel her eyes on us while we're doing something we know to stop before she becomes upset. But sometimes we're too late. Her voice erupts in hot waves from her throat, foaming in spittle at the edges of her lips. Her voice rises to the ceiling and hangs there, hovering above everything, and her sweat drips from her forehead and we stare ahead, trying to show her our love with our silence. Sometimes she gets it, she receives it, and her anger dissipates above us and her sweat cools and sinks into her face, and then she smiles and everything becomes still.

Usually, though, she doesn't get it. She takes our silence personally, she forgets her lifelong lesson to us, and she yells until she's exhausted herself. Then she sits against the wall and cries. My brother and I carry blankets from our side of the room and cover her with them, and we burrow in on each side of her. This, too, is love.

I dreamed constantly at the shelter. Dreaming was the same to me, no matter the time of day, whether my eyes were opened or closed. I could maintain a dream through the day if I woke myself up, so I tried to rise as early as possible each morning in order to preserve my connection to the other side.

I dreamed as I rubbed my eyes and went to the bathroom. I dreamed as I brushed my teeth and took a shower. I dreamed as I woke my mother and brother, as we started our day together.

I saw my father in the mirror as I brushed my teeth. He

looked just like me, with his wide nose, his proud forehead. I nodded solemnly at him, and he nodded back. Instead of sitting on the floor with our breakfast I knew we were actually sitting on a brand-new couch, and my father's favorite Sunny Ade record was playing, and our silence was laughter. When Mom pinched me up and down my back her hands became warm and supple. She embraced me through the punishment. Her slaps were a burst of hot water on my face. My tears were the drops trailing down my face after the water had hit the floor. Each slap made me clean. Her eyes seemed angry because they were so red. I reached forward with my magic eraser and erased all the red until her eyes were white again. When I was finished her anger was finished.

I soared, and I swam, and I dunked basketballs. No one ever told me that I was supposed to differentiate what I saw during the night from what I saw during the day, that I should privilege one over the other, so everything converged. I grew to believe that pain was temporary, that I was only a few steps from learning how to fly. I knew I would grow wings. It was only a matter of time.

My brother and I didn't see our father for three months. A few days after we arrived at the shelter Mom told us that our father would be coming to live with us soon. A few weeks into our stay, though, she told us he didn't want to live with us anymore, so we probably wouldn't see him ever again. We didn't believe her. We knew too much about our father's love for us to believe he had simply abandoned us.

One day, finally, the white lady with the freckles appeared and told us we would be seeing Dad soon. She told us we would only be able to see him on weekends, because that's what the judge had said. Who is the judge? we wondered. "Don't worry," she replied, "just know that you will be safe. We will protect you."

I had no idea what she was talking about. I had never felt unsafe with my father. I was upset that I didn't have a chance to speak with the judge. I wanted to go on TV and talk to Judge Wapner from *The People's Court*. I knew if I had a few minutes with him I could convince him that our family needed to be together again.

We met Dad in the common area of the shelter. He was crying.

"How are you doing?" he asked us. "How have you been? Have they been taking care of you?"

We were upset with him.

"Why didn't you come for us before? Why did you leave us here? Where were you?"

Dad extended his hands helplessly.

"I don't know. I am here now."

My brother gave him a big hug, and I couldn't resist either. Dad held both of our hands and I turned to see Mom stewing at us from the corner of the room. Dad told her he'd have us back by Sunday. Mom turned and walked away.

Our apartment felt strange though it looked exactly the same. Dad had even left our toys on the ground where we'd discarded them the morning we were taken to the shelter. For a moment we just stood there, looking at each other. Then Dad flipped on the TV and asked us to sit on his lap.

That Saturday Hulk Hogan looked into our living room and told us to eat our vitamins, say our prayers, and listen to our parents. He was so big. Then we saw him wrestle. He was fighting a large, fearsome opponent, and he was winning, but then another wrestler jumped into the ring and punched the referee. He punched Hulk. Hulk was down on the mat, grimacing in pain, and the mysterious wrestler disappeared. Hulk's opponent hit him repeatedly on the head, and then he pinned him. We were silent, my brother, Dad, and I, as Hulk lay on the mat, bleeding, on the verge of losing the match. But then he reached his hand to the sky and began to shake it. He shook his hand until the power from the sky seemed to course through his fingers into his arms and into his body. He shook like a new force was inside him, and he rose slowly from the canvas. He kept shaking even as his opponent beat him on the face and chest, and then he made a great fist of both of his hands and slammed it down on his opponent's back. His opponent collapsed, and a few moments later the newly revived referee raised Hulk's arm in victory. We cheered and hugged each other. After my father tucked us in that night I spent hours with my hand raised to the ceiling, shaking it, waiting for the mysterious power to enter my body.

The next day we sat and talked, but in the evening Dad told us we would have to go back to the shelter. We begged him to let us stay for just a few hours more, but he said it wasn't possible. We bundled into the car and he drove us back. We saw Mom as we were walking in, and she took our hands without saying anything to Dad. We heard him talking behind us.

"Theresa, what are you doing?"

Silence.

"Why are you trying to take my kids away? Why are you breaking up our family?"

Silence.

I don't remember talking much with my brother during this period. I'm sure we spoke often, but the words we exchanged are forever lost to me. I spent most of my time looking out for him. I talked to him under my breath through the long silences, and I shielded him whenever Mom reached for us in anger. I was glad that my mother took her anger out on me. I actually felt like a big boy when she raised my arm and pinched me down my side and back, gathering my skin between her nails and pressing as hard as she could each time. The welts were hot and red. Sometimes I counted them and wondered how many should have been for him.

After a while, though, I noticed that my mother stopped reaching for my brother altogether. She always lunged for me, even if she was angry with him.

And then she stopped being angry with my brother.

When she beat me she would sometimes call me by my father's name. I didn't know how to respond, and when I tried to tell her that I wasn't my father she beat me harder.

"Stop denying yourself," she would say between slaps.

"Stop trying to be something you aren't," she would say while pinching me.

I never told anyone what my mother was doing to me. I believed that my silence was a part of my maturity. If I told anyone, I would be admitting that I wasn't an adult. I don't know if my tutor or Joy ever suspected what was happening to me, but they were nicer to me as time passed; I received more hugs and kisses than any other kid in the shelter.

One night, after pinching me all over my back, Mom asked me if I loved her. I gave her a big hug and told my brother to join us. We sat there on the floor hugging for a long while, and then Mom told us that it was almost time for her to leave.

"Where are you going?" we asked her.

"I am too sick for this world," she said. "I won't be here for much longer."

"Will you take me with you?" my brother asked expectantly.

She shook her head slowly. "No. I wish I could, but no."

About a week before it happened, Mom came into the living room and saw me sitting on the floor. I was exhausted. It was dark outside, and the window was open. My brother was sleeping on a mat on the other side of the room. Mom smiled as she approached me. A little of the moonlight touched her face.

I began to shiver because I thought she was going to hit me again. When she sat next to me I sneezed in fear. She raised her hand and I bowed my head, waiting for the hard sting of her hand against my face. Instead she rubbed my cheek. I began to cry. I was so relieved.

"What is wrong with you?" Mom asked. I didn't respond. She held my hand.

"I just want you to know, I don't hate you," she whispered. "I hate your father."

I didn't say a word.

"I hate him for bringing me here, and I hate him for giving me hope."

I nodded.

"But you're too much like him," she said. "And that is why you and I can never be friends."

I looked up at her.

"One day you will understand," she said. "Everything that I have done will make sense. You will see."

I nodded again. Mom kissed my cheek. Then she got up and left.

Mom began to take her pills more frequently, soon every hour, and then every few minutes. One evening, while she was preparing our fried chicken, she dropped the package of aluminum foil on the floor, whirled around, and opened the cabinet above the fridge. She pulled a new bottle of pills from inside, flipped the top, and shoved everything down her throat, cotton balls and all. I remember her choking on the cotton balls, and falling to her hands and knees to retrieve the pills she had spit up. She crawled on the floor, saliva dripping from her mouth, slurping the yellow and red pills from the wood floor like an anteater. My brother and I watched her until she was done. When she had slurped down the last pill she leaned her body against the wall and smiled at us.

"That was fun," she said.

She just sat there for a while. Then she started nodding off. My brother ran over to her and began tapping, then shaking her so she would stay awake. The oven started smoking, big noxious fumes, and soon we were all coughing, except for Mom. I ran out of the room and looked for Joy.

My father picked us up the following morning. When we arrived at our apartment he did not comfort us or ask us any questions, he just told us to change our clothes. My brother and I became scared.

"Where are we going?"

"Don't worry, just hurry up."

I started to cry. My brother ran off to our bedroom. We were still traumatized by what we had seen the night before, the strangers bending over Mom, Joy whisking us away and telling us Mom was fine even though we had seen her lying still, three or four cotton balls scattered around her. Dad called my brother back to the living room and smiled at us.

"Come on now! Get ready! I promise we'll have fun!"

My brother and I changed and followed Dad to the car. We drove for a few minutes and then we stopped in front of my old school, the school I had attended for just a few weeks before Mom took us away. The school I hadn't seen in over a year.

"You will be going back there soon." my father said, pointing. "Prepare yourself now. I expect both of you to be the best students in the school. There will be no excuses."

We sat staring at the brick building. I read the sign in the parking lot, next to the flagpole. It said: HAPPY THANKS-GIVING! SCHOOL RESUMES NOVEMBER 28TH.

Dad then drove us to the mall. He bought cinnamon rolls for us and we sat on a bench near a department store. We saw all the moms and dads bustling from store to store with massive bags in their hands, some carrying, others dragging their children behind them. We saw a fake star affixed to a fake tree, and fake snow that was spread all over the fake presents below. I knew better than to ask Dad about our own Christmas presents. We munched on our rolls.

Dad drove us back to the shelter the following week. Mom smiled weakly when she saw us.

"My sons. I have missed you."

She hugged each of us, and she held me longer than usual.

"I am very sorry. I love you, my child."

She held our hands and we walked slowly back to our room.

"I have a very special surprise for both of you. Close your eyes."

I felt her pushing something warm into my hands. I looked down and saw a plate with two pieces of oven-ready fried chicken, some green beans, Chinese rice, and a Santa Claus cookie on the side. He had an M&M nose and a beard of frosting.

We ate in silence.

The courtroom was much bigger than I thought it would be. I couldn't imagine how they fit everything inside the TV.

Everyone was quiet as my brother and I walked in. It was the first time I remember wearing a suit.

How did we get here? I don't know. There are too many pages of memory missing.

The judge was an old white man, but he wasn't Judge Wapner, or the judge from the other show we used to watch with Joy. He smiled at my brother and me.

"Don't be scared or nervous. We are all here because we want the best for you," he said.

Something happened after this, I'm not sure what. And then the judge slowly swings his head—a massive, bearded pendulum—back in our direction.

"This could go on forever," he says. "But I think you guys know who you want to be with. I can't promise that I will do as you ask me, but I will weigh your words very carefully."

My brother looks at me and I feel my face burning.

I look down at my shoes, and then I look up at the judge, his head shifting almost imperceptibly from left to right and back again, like it's keeping time.

"I want to stay with my father."

"Are you sure?"

"Yes, I'm sure."

"And you?"

We both look at my brother and he nods.

Sometimes when I close my eyes and travel back to that bewildering time I see Mom shaking her head at me, shooting me hateful glances as we pack our things from her room and leave the shelter for the last time. Usually, though, she isn't there. Not even her ghost greets me, not even a blast of cold air. She disappears from the story. She simply evaporates.

I am both ashamed and not ashamed to say that I did not miss her initially. I just wanted to fly away, to leave all my sadness behind.

My mother lives in Nigeria now, and I know almost nothing about her life. Who she is, what she does, what she hopes to be. I haven't seen her since she left. I don't know if I'll ever see her again.

There are so many questions I would like to ask her.

When I think of her now, I think of the old white lady who used to accompany me to school each day. When I told my father that I wanted to serve her in heaven, he wrung his hands and shook his head. He told me I would serve no one but God, and then he called my mother and asked her to walk me to school the following day. "It'll be good for you to leave the house for a bit," he said to her.

As Mom, my brother, and I walked together Mrs. Hansen materialized beside us, and she told my mother that she, too, could serve her in heaven. Years later I learned that Mrs. Hansen was referencing an old notion of the Mormon church, that black people, sons and daughters of Cain, could only get to heaven as servants.

Mom stopped and touched her face. She smiled warmly and told her that we would all be together in heaven as equals, all our earthly worries behind us forever, and wasn't that such a wonderful thing? Mrs. Hansen nodded, and then she smiled like something joyous and satisfying had just occurred to her. She slowly tottered away, and I never saw her again.

I remember Mom smiling triumphantly as we walked the rest of the way to school, her face lovely and calm. She seemed perfect to me then.

GRANDMA + TUNDE

Dad held the phone close to his ear, and then he dialed some numbers. There were so many. I was amazed he could remember all of them.

He said he was calling Grandma. I had only spoken to her once, and I wasn't sure what I was supposed to say, so I didn't say much. I'd never spoken to her until Mom left.

Dad started talking to Grandma. He yelled at her. But I knew his yelling wasn't a bad yelling, like Mom used to yell. He smiled while he yelled, so I knew he was happy, or he was trying to be happy.

He gave me the phone. He smiled at me. My hand shook a little.

"Hello?"

"Hello, my son! How are you?"

I was confused because she called me her son. I looked at Dad but I guess he read my mind because he nodded. "Keep talking," he whispered.

"I am fine."

"How is your daddy doing?"

"He is doing fine."

"Are you taking care of him?"

"I can't take care of him! He's my dad."

"Yes, but you are becoming a big boy, so you have to learn how to take care of him."

"Yes, ma."

"Hello?"

"Hello."

"Can you hear me?"

"It's hard."

"OK, I can hear you now. How is the weather over there?"

I looked out the window and saw the snow everywhere. It had been snowing for many days.

"It's snowing."

"Snowing? Describe the snow for me. How is it?"

"It's white."

"Is it like rain?"

"Yes. It's like white rain."

"Does it feel wet when it falls on your face?"

I closed my eyes and tried to remember how the snow felt on my face.

"At first it feels like wet tissue paper, and then it feels like water."

"Do you like the snow?"

"It's OK."

"What are you doing to prepare for Christmas?"

"We aren't doing anything."

I looked around to see if my father was still listening. He was sitting with Tayo on the floor, whispering something in his ear.

"I want Santa to bring us some presents, but I don't think he will this year."

"Well, if you are good, Father Christmas will bring you some presents."

"Who is Father Christmas?"

"He is Santa's older brother. He is very nice. He always finds a way to give gifts to children who do not receive presents from Santa."

I was so happy that my face felt hot. I never even knew that Father Christmas existed. I started to think about all the presents I would ask Father Christmas for when my father took the phone and gave it to Tayo. I ran to my room and closed my eyes and thanked God that He gave Santa a nice older brother who cared about poor children like me.

In the living room I heard Dad hanging up the phone. That's when I remembered that I forgot to ask Grandma about Mommy.

1988–91

The most confusing period of my childhood began when my mother left us and returned to Nigeria. She left without any warning—one day, after we returned home from school, Dad told my brother and me that we would not be seeing Mom for a while because she was flying in a big plane back to Lagos. I wasn't sure what to say. Part of me was relieved; Tayo and I had seen her only once since the hearing, and I didn't really want to go back to the shelter because I was afraid she would hurt me again. Maybe going back to Nigeria was some kind of punishment, like the time I had to stand in the corner after stealing a cookie from the pantry. The other part of me was devastated. How could she leave without saying goodbye? I looked up at Dad and he smiled. Then he shrugged. He kissed my forehead. "She will be back soon," he said. "There's nothing to worry about."

I was seven and my brother was five. I hadn't yet learned that sometimes adults say things just to say things. That sometimes they were just as confused as you.

In the days following Mom's departure my father assumed the guise of a superhero. He kept hunger at bay by working longer hours as a mechanic at various shops across northern Utah. He fought off the forces of sadness by laughing at everything, no matter how bleak or obscene. He vanquished our fears by telling Tayo and me that he would always be there for us, no matter what. And he taught us the meaning of kindness by never once uttering a negative word about our mother.

For a time we lived this way, my father laughing, dancing, working, teasing, praying. He told us that Mom was receiving special care in Nigeria, and that she was getting better every day. Tayo and I imagined tall, good-looking doctors standing over her with notepads and clipboards, almost like the doctors we'd seen on TV (unlike the doctors on Dad's favorite show, *M*A*S*H*, our imaginary doctors were black, and they spoke Yoruba to each other as they attended to Mom).

As time passed, though, my brother and I began to notice a change in Dad. He seemed less confident than he'd been before. He maintained his habit of chasing us around our little apartment before leaving for work each morning, but now instead of tickling us at the end he hugged each of us fiercely, and he didn't let go until we tapped him on the shoulder and called his name. He still told us he loved us at least twice a day, but the way he said it sometimes made us feel as if he were saying it for the last time.

Sometimes, when we stood by his bedroom door, we heard him praying quietly, insistently, begging God to make Mom right.

One night, after Mom had been gone a month or so, my father tucked Tayo and me in and closed the door without saying a word to us. After a few minutes we heard him sniffling in the living room. Tayo got up and walked to the door, and I followed. When we reached the living room we saw Dad sitting on the couch with his head in his hands. Tayo tapped his shoulder and Dad looked up at us. His eyes were red, and his mustache was wet. He shook his head slowly. I suddenly felt very queasy. "Mom isn't coming back," he said. I looked down at his feet. He'd been wearing the same pair of socks for four days; I knew this because his big toes were sticking through each one. "She is just too sick. This country's no good for her."

We tried to get more information from him, but Dad began to speak in riddles, as he often did when he didn't feel like telling us anything more. When we asked him why America was no good for her, he told us that we had eyes at the front of our heads for a reason. When we asked him what he meant by that, he told us to go back to sleep.

Tayo and I returned to our bedroom and sat on our beds.

"How can Mom still be sick?" Tayo asked. "She's been gone forever."

"Yeah," I agreed.

Tayo kicked the air, and his foot fell back to the side of his bed with a soft thud.

"I'm scared," Tayo said.

I just nodded.

In the weeks that followed, Dad stopped playing with us, and he sent us to bed early each night. Afterward, he would stay up and yell at the telephone—we knew he was talking to someone in Nigeria whenever he did that. We could never make out what he was saying, but we wondered if he was speaking to Mom. We wondered if Mom was trying to convince Dad that she needed to come back. If Dad was telling her to give America one last chance.

In time, Mom's absence became the most prominent aspect our lives. Dad stopped talking about her, and he encouraged us to do the same, but we could tell he missed her. Sometimes he'd slip up and tell us to ask Mom what she was preparing for dinner. Other times, when we passed by his bedroom on the way to the bathroom, we saw him fingering some of the items she'd left behind. Her purse. Her records. Her colorful head wraps. Her purple flip-flops.

Tayo and I continued to speak about Mom, but we always whispered when we did so, like she was a secret that only he and I shared. Like her life was a story we had made up.

One spring morning, maybe four or five months after Mom returned to Nigeria, my father strode into our bedroom while Tayo and I were getting dressed for school. He sat on Tayo's bed, which was closest to the door.

"Come here," he said.

I joined Tayo and my father on the bed.

"I know you guys miss Mom very much. And I know you guys want to talk to her. But she can't talk to you now. And it's possible you won't talk to her for a very long time."

"What do you mean?" asked Tayo.

"Let me finish," Dad said. He smiled and then he coughed. He took off his glasses and rubbed his eyes.

"You guys are both young, but there are certain things that you need to know. Life doesn't always go the way you want it to, but God always has a plan for us. And it's not our job to question His plan. Do you understand?"

"Yes, sah," we both said.

"Good. Things are going to change from now on. And it may be difficult in the beginning. But everything is going to work out."

With that, Dad reached into the front pocket of his overalls and pulled out a small picture. He gave it to me. The lady in the picture was beautiful—she had a round nose, deep dimples, and bronze skin.

I did not know who she was.

"This is your new mother," my father said, solemnly. "I am going to Nigeria to pick her up next month. She is from Lagos, like me, and she's ready to meet you guys."

We couldn't believe it. We hadn't expected anything like this.

"Who is she?' I asked. 'And what about—"

"Everything is going to be fine. Don't worry. Finish getting dressed."

He got up and left the room.

Tayo began to cry. I moved closer to him and rubbed his back. And then I began to cry as well.

Dad flew to Nigeria two weeks later. He left a picture of our new mom for us, and I spent hours after school looking at it. I tried my best to see this stranger as a member of our family, but it was hard. I couldn't imagine her preparing moin moin the way my mother had when she felt like cooking. I couldn't imagine feeling as safe in her arms as I'd felt in my mother's arms, even when I knew she was only holding me so she could pinch me up and down my back and legs. Even though the only evidence I had of my mother's love were the scars she'd engraved on my body.

My brother and I stayed with an older white couple while Dad was gone. They lived in a large redbrick house on the other side of town. Dad dropped us off on his way to the airport, and after introducing us to them he rushed back to his car and waved good-bye before revving the engine and speeding off. Tayo and I stood on their porch waving even after his car had disappeared from view.

The old lady stood there with us, her hands on our shoulders. I'd never seen her in my life. She was taller than Dad, and I remember being fascinated by her long, silvery hair. She was the first old person I'd seen with long hair. I'd always thought that people couldn't grow long hair after a certain age.

She gave Tayo and me a hug after Dad disappeared, then she stepped back and stared at us for a moment.

"Welcome to my home," she said. "You can call me Missy."

She smiled, and then she turned and walked into her house. Tayo rubbed his arms behind her back, like he was trying to rub her hug away. I glared at him and he stopped.

I'd never been inside a white person's house before, and everything I saw assumed a special meaning. In the corner of their living room a tall grandfather clock stood staring at me. I heard it ticking under its breath. There were pictures all over the walls, and the people in them looked so happy that I wanted to step into the pictures and sit with them, so I could smile at whatever they were smiling at. Tayo rushed across the room and picked up a small globe that was sitting on a side table next to their dark leather couch. He stared at it as if he expected the miniature people inside to wave at him. I glared at him again but then I looked up to see Missy smiling as she whooshed by me. She took the globe from his hands and showed him how, by shaking it for just a few seconds, he could initiate a small, furious snowstorm, a beautiful blizzard encased in glass. I was jealous as I stood there by myself, watching Tayo shake the globe again and again as Missy nodded her approval. Yet I was happy, too, because I could still smell her. Her scent had remained with me after she rushed by to show Tayo the secret of the globe. She smelled like something soft, like my mother's favorite perfume.

That night, after a dinner of fried fish and rice, the old man showed us our room. I could just make out the fading striped wallpaper in the dim light. The dry carpet scratched my bare feet. The beds were small and thin. Tayo and I stared up at the man, and he smiled. He had a thick white mustache, and he was missing a few teeth.

"You think you guys will be OK here by yourself?" he asked.

We nodded.

"Let me know if you need anything. You can call me Mr. Devlin." He rubbed my head. "We're happy to have you. Your father's a good man," he said. Then he closed the door behind him.

Tayo and I didn't say a word until we had changed into our pajamas and I flipped off the light.

"When do you think Daddy's coming back?" he asked.

"I don't know."

"Soon?"

"I don't know."

"Do you think he'll come back with Mom?"

"I don't know."

"What will happen to Mom if he comes back with a new Mom?"

"I don't know."

"Why don't you know anything?"

"I don't know."

"Tunde!"

I laughed.

"I hope he comes back with Mom, but I like it here," he said.

I paused for a moment.

"Me too."

A few days after we moved in with the old couple I mentioned to them—over a big dinner of turkey, stuffing, and green beans, food that I'd only seen on the television before then—that I loved to read books about karate. Missy leaned over her plate and asked me if I had ever been to a karate class. I told her my father believed that karate was violent, that he had told me he would never allow me to learn. She smiled widely at me. The next day she picked me up from school and took me straight to a karate studio, and for two hours I kicked, punched, screeched, and had a wonderful time. She took me to karate class almost every day after that, and when I wasn't practicing kicks and punches around their house, Tayo and I played together in their den, which had a massive TV with dozens of animated movies stacked in neat piles on top.

It seemed like Missy and Mr. Devlin loved us from the moment we arrived. They took us to movies and puppet shows and bought candy for us. They taught us nursery rhymes and fed us strange foods that we learned to love. We went to church with them on Sundays, and they held our hands as we sat on the hard pews. Missy hugged and kissed us more than our parents ever did, and I sometimes wondered if she were actually my grandmother, if maybe we had other white relatives that my father had never told us about.

As our days became weeks Tayo and I missed Dad more than we could have imagined, especially when we didn't hear from him. But we couldn't believe that we were living such joy-filled, impossible lives.

After we'd been living with them for about a month, though, Missy and Mr. Devlin began to treat us differently. They began to send us straight to bed after dinner without reading to us. They began to ask us odd questions.

"Did your daddy tell you when he was coming back?" Mr. Devlin asked, his bushy eyebrows making him seem for all the world like a cartoon character come to life.

"Did your daddy say anything about what he was planning to do in Africa?' Missy asked, peering at us like one of those angry witches from our favorite Disney movies.

I nodded emphatically at this question and showed them

the picture of our new mom. Missy looked at it for a long time before placing the small picture back in my hand.

"Who is this?" she said.

"That's our new mom," said Tayo.

Missy's eyes grew wide. She touched Mr. Devlin's side and they stepped away from our bedroom. They began to whisper to each other. I could not hear much, but I heard Missy say "no divorce," and "good woman." After a few minutes they came back. Missy smiled kindly at me.

"I'm afraid that your father lied to us," she said. "He lied to us about what he was doing in Africa. He lied about how long he would be there. I'm afraid that you and your brother can't live here anymore."

The following morning, Missy woke us up early and drove us to a tall white building a few blocks away. She held our hands as we walked inside and asked us to sit on the couch near the door. She approached a short lady with black hair who was standing behind a big wooden desk on the other side of the room. She occasionally pointed to us as she spoke with the lady, and then she walked back to us, kissed each of us on the forehead, and left. She drove away.

The short lady with black hair was nice; she allowed us to play with the toys that were scattered about the room. Tayo and I couldn't answer any of the questions she asked us. That evening she drove us to another house and introduced us to a younger white couple. The woman with the black hair told us that they were our foster parents, that they would take care of us until our daddy came back.

———

Dad returned from Nigeria two days after we moved in with our foster parents. He simply showed up one afternoon after school and picked us up.

"Daddy, what about our foster parents?" I asked as we entered the car.

"Don't worry about them," he replied gruffly. "I am your father, not them."

We drove in silence for a few minutes, and then Tayo spoke up from the backseat.

"Is our new mom at home?"

"No."

"Is she coming soon?"

"No."

"What about Mom? Is she coming back?"

"No, and don't ask me any more questions about her. Don't worry about her. Kick her out of your memory."

Dad looked angry, so we listened to him.

Things went back to normal. Dad never told us why he was late in returning from Nigeria, and he didn't mention anything about our new mom again.

My father changed jobs a few weeks later, and then he changed jobs again. We saw him even less than before, but he began to talk to us for long periods of time at random moments; sometimes after we'd finished our dinner, sometimes before he left for work, sometimes after he'd tucked us in.

"I have big dreams for both of you," he'd say. "You guys are the only reason I am still in this country. I should have left a long time ago, because I don't have any opportunities here. No one takes me seriously. But whenever I think of leaving I ask myself what the both of you would be like if you grew up in Nigeria. Here you can become leaders. I don't know what would happen there."

We always nodded, but I can't say that I really understood what he was talking about. Nigeria, to me, to us, was merely a chorus of scratchy voices over the telephone, a collection of foods and customs that our friends had never heard of. It was a place where everyone was black, where our cousins spoke a language we couldn't fully comprehend. Where our mother lived.

But somehow I knew that my father was right. And I was glad we were living in America. In Utah. I never wanted to be anywhere else.

After Dad tucked us in, Tayo and I would stay up and read to each other. We waited until we saw the thin patch of light beneath our door go dark, until we heard Dad's soft snores rattling down the hallway. Then Tayo would reach under his bed, pull out our emergency flashlight, and walk over to the single, tall bookshelf on the other side of our room.

We had dozens of books. My father never bought us toys, and he always claimed that he was too broke to buy us new clothes, but somehow we each received at least three new books each month. Most of our books were nonfiction—short biographies, children's encyclopedias, textbooks—because Dad was convinced that novels were for entertainment purposes only, and he always told us that we would have time for entertainment when we were old enough to make our own decisions. So Tayo and I would huddle in a single bed, his or mine, with a biography about George Washington, or a book about the invention of the telephone, and each of us would read a page and hand the flashlight over.

We eventually grew tired of these books, though, so we began to make up our own stories. Actually, Tayo made them up. Even though Tayo was younger than me, even though he looked up to me and followed me in every other part of our lives, he was a much better storyteller than I was. He was almost as good as Mom.

He always began:

"Once upon a time . . ."

"There was . . ."

"There was a large elephant with a long purple nose and polka-dot underwear . . ."

"That liked to run . . ."

"That liked to run all over the valleys and desert, and the elephant had many friends, giraffes and leopards, and a cranky orangutan that always wore a pair of bifocals like Dad's . . ."

We'd continue in this manner, sometimes for an hour or more, until Tayo fell asleep. Then I'd pull the flashlight from his hands, place it back under his bed, and snuggle in next to him.

One Saturday morning, as Tayo and I were playing basketball on the concrete courts behind our apartment building, laughing, shouting, and leaping, Tayo stopped dribbling and looked up at me, his eyes shining, hopeful.

"Don't you wish Mom would come back?" he asked.

I didn't know what to say. I took my status as older brother seriously, and I knew that Tayo would probably mimic whatever I said. I wasn't sure if it would be OK for me to tell the truth, or if I was supposed to say what Dad would say in this situation. I chose something in the middle.

"Sometimes," I said.

"I do all the time," Tayo said. "I want her to come back now."

And a part of me agreed with him. I wanted her to come back, I wanted everything to be the way it had been before she got sick. Before she left us.

But the other part . . .

Looking back, I think I was open to the idea of a new mom because there was a part of me that was ready to consign my mother to memory. I wanted to install a false version of her in my mind. I wanted to forgive her by forgetting her cruelty, the pinching, the slapping, the screaming. I wanted to forgive her by forgetting her.

But now, Mom, I remember your hugs. They were warm and tight. When you wrapped your arms around me I always felt as if I was home. And your food was delicious. Even when you stopped cooking, even when you would only warm up a few pieces of frozen chicken in the oven and open up cans of beans and corn for dinner, your food tasted as if you'd spent hours preparing it.

And your smiles; I will always remember your smiles. They were rare and lovely, like priceless coins from an ancient kingdom.

Our new mom finally arrived in August of 1991, almost three years after our mother returned to Nigeria, and a few months after we moved from Bountiful to a small apartment in nearby Hartville. Tayo and I didn't know who she was—Dad told us she was not the same woman he'd visited in Nigeria before. My father had flown back to Nigeria right after I completed second grade, and this time he dropped Tayo and me off with the foster family we'd stayed with once. They took us in without any questions, and Dad promised them he would be back in a month. When he returned—this time after only a couple weeks—he informed us that we had to prepare for the arrival of our new mother. We excitedly cleaned everything—our walls, our floors, our tables, our chairs—and asked him for more details about her. How does she look? "You'll see," he said, preparing our food as Sunny Ade sang sweetly to us from the living room. What does she do, we asked as we did our homework. "She'll tell you," he replied as he cleaned the stove. Will she love us, we asked as he tucked us in. "How couldn't she?" he said before kissing each of us on the forehead and turning off the light. He gave us the same ambiguous responses each time we asked about her, and after a few weeks we stopped believing that she was even real. But on the day of her arrival he told us that we would have a new mother by the evening.

"She is a good woman," he said. "Trust me."

There were other questions I wanted to ask. Why did we

need someone else? After all, we already had something special. After months of disorientation we had finally managed to fashion a new family from the wreckage of what had been before. I was beginning to understand that a family could be something more than a group of people who were supposed to stay together despite the pain they caused each other. My brother and I were living in a single-parent home, and our father was rarely around, but we were as happy as we had ever been.

Why did anything have to change? How did we know this would even work?

And what about our mother, our real mother? I didn't know what I was supposed to do with all the love I had for her, pulsing inside me.

But then I remembered what my father had said when we'd asked about her before—that we had eyes at the front our heads for a reason. I suddenly understood what he meant: he wanted us to keep looking forward, no matter what, to keep moving, to overcome our pain by acting as if pain was something temporary and easily forgotten. He was my father, and I loved and trusted him, so I tried my best to heed his advice. I didn't know how much anguish I would cause myself by doing this.

Much later I would come to understand that the only way my father had survived in the United States, in Utah, was by doing exactly this: staring ahead always, kicking the pain and heartache away. This was how he was able to survive the torment of living in a place that never fully comprehended his presence, that sometimes treated him as if he were someone who would never really matter. This was how he survived the loss of his wife to a disease that prevented her from remembering him, and his love for her, for more than a moment at a time. My father bore his burdens well; he was a walking, talking smile. But now, knowing what I know, and feeling as I do, I can only imagine what was actually happening inside. It makes me wonder how well I know him, if he is actually the person who raised me, who hugs me so warmly when I see him today.

We drove to the airport in Salt Lake City that evening, and Dad told Tayo and me to wait in the car. After he'd walked a few feet he turned around and looked down at me in the passenger seat. "You're going to have to move to the back," he said, and I saw something like sadness glimmering from his eyes. I moved as quickly as I could, but he ignored the smile I flashed at him after I'd settled in the backseat. He stood there looking at Tayo and me for a few minutes, but even as he looked at us it seemed like he was staring at something far away, something we would never see no matter how long and hard we tried. Then he shook his head slowly and his eyes began to tear up. He turned around and walked away.

Twenty minutes later we saw Dad approaching with a tall woman beside him and a young child walking slightly in front of them. The woman was carrying another child.

Tayo and I stared at each other. We were shocked. Dad hadn't mentioned anything about kids. When the woman arrived at my window she reached down from the sky and took my hand into hers. She stared deep into my eyes. Her eyes were large, brown, and oval. I saw something like love flickering faintly from them. She smiled. I smiled back.

"Hello," she said. "It is wonderful to meet you."

The two children scampered into the backseat with us. They were wearing clothes just like ours, T-shirts and white-washed jeans. They didn't acknowledge our presence. The older one looked sullenly ahead and the younger one tucked himself into a ball and began to suck his thumb. Dad settled into the driver's seat and appraised us in the rearview mirror.

"How is my new family doing!" he boomed, and he started the car. As we drove out of the parking lot he slipped his right hand into the left hand of the woman.

Our New Mom seemed surprised when we arrived at our apartment. She placed her bags down at the threshold and looked left and right as if she was searching for something. She looked at Dad.

"Where . . ." she began, and then she walked over to the sink and grabbed a pair of bright yellow cleaning gloves from the middle of the drain board. She wiped her face with her forearm and pulled the gloves on. Then she reached into the cabinet, pulled out a bucket, and filled it with soap and water. We were all watching her as she placed the bucket on the floor and got on her hands and knees.

"Join me," she said simply.

We were bewildered. The little one continued to suck his thumb. Dad looked deflated, as if her words had deprived him of air.

Now she scrubbed the floor with a sponge I'd never seen

before, and my eyes opened to a different apartment. The floor resembled a painting I had once seen on television, on a show hosted by a man who violently attacked a blank canvas with vibrant colors, as if he were at war with it. When the host finished Dad scoffed at the finished product, those intersecting jagged lines of color. "That isn't art," he said. Our floor looked exactly the same. It wasn't art. Our walls were even worse—handprints, bug corpses, the remains of bug corpses, stains of indeterminate origin—maybe it *was* art. A portrait of our poverty.

Tayo walked to the sink and retrieved another sponge, and he bent down to work. Soon the older one bent down too, and then I joined them. Only Dad and the little one stood together, and as I glanced up at them I noticed, for the first time, how similar they looked. Dad was short and thick, like the little one, and their faces held the same features in the same proportion. They were both frowning now, and Dad's frown, spreading slowly over the lower half of his face, was a larger copy of the little one's frown. Dad stared at us.

"Do we have to do this now? You just arrived! Change your clothes! Go take a shower! I have already prepared a meal for you. And we have already cleaned the house! We can clean some more in the morning!"

New Mom looked up.

"I will not be showering in this filthy apartment. Come and help us clean. Or if you are too tired you can go lie down and I will tell you when we are finished so we can eat together."

She returned to her cleaning and the rest of us looked at Dad to see what he would do. He sheepishly reached over our heads for a rag and went to work on the walls.

We cleaned for about two hours, and at the end our apartment looked better. But not quite clean. I felt ashamed of our apartment for the first time, and I wondered how it appeared to my new brothers, fresh from their trip across the sea. New Mom rose to her feet and smiled broadly.

"Now we can eat," she said, and she turned to the stove. She laughed when she saw what was inside the pots.

"Let me work on this for a moment. I will tell you when I'm finished," she said.

The rest of us moved to the living room. A few minutes later I smelled the mingling aromas of tomatoes and onions and peppers. We sat there staring awkwardly at each other for half an hour until New Mom called for us.

There were six steaming plates of fufu and chicken stew on the table. We sat and my father asked us to hold hands. New Mom was sitting next to me, and she squeezed my hand every few seconds as Dad prayed. When he finished she winked at me. Then we dug in. The food was beautiful and good. We all smacked loudly, and then we all went to bed.

That night I felt the older one pressing his knees into my back as I tried to rock myself to sleep. At dinner Dad had informed Tayo and me that we would have to share our beds with our new brothers until he could afford to buy new beds. When we arrived at our bedroom the little one plopped onto the bottom bunk of the bunk bed I shared with Tayo, and when I tried to get in with him he began to scream. Dad and New Mom rushed in, and Dad shook his head after the little one pointed a miniature accusatory finger at me.

"You have already started trouble?" he said, and when I protested he yelled over me:

"They have just arrived after flying for godknowshow-many miles, and now you want to prevent them from sleeping? What is wrong with you?" I looked around to see who he was talking to. My father was still staring at me when I glanced at him once more. I was confused. My father had never spoken to me this way.

The little one fell asleep shortly after Dad and New Mom left, and Tayo crawled into bed with him. The little one turned around and hugged Tayo tight around the neck. I climbed up to the top bunk and the older one followed me. We soon began a war for space.

We traded subtle elbows and knee jabs until he fell asleep against my back. I tried, inch by inch, to push him out of the bed, but I became tired myself, and I fell asleep too.

New Mom woke me up the following morning and I saw her face up close for the first time. She had large, open, even features. Her wide nose was framed by ample cheeks, and her hairline was beginning to leak into the top part of her forehead. I woke up my brother and stepbrothers, and we all sat around the dining table and introduced ourselves to each other. I learned that the little one was called Ade, and the older one was called Femi. Femi resembled his mother more than Ade, but they both had her nose and small ears, and when they smiled it was hard to tell them apart. For some reason I was surprised that they spoke English so well. Dad must have been listening in on my thoughts because he looked over at me and said,

"Yes, they are very smart! You know that in Nigeria the early school system is much better than it is here. Both of them will probably end up skipping some grades. They may be smarter than you!"

At this he laughed and New Mom looked down with embarrassed pride. I scowled at the table.

Our first few days together were consumed with the business of becoming a family. We threw out countless articles of clothing and various knickknacks. We went to the department store and purchased new drapes, sheets, and comforters. New Mom threw out all of our pots. By the evening she had us cleaning again, and by the following morning we started to become more comfortable with one another. Mom came up with nicknames for Tayo and I—she called me "thick eyes" because of my glasses, and she called Tayo "handsome."

GRANDMA + TUNDE

"Hello, Grandma."

"Who is this?"

"It's Tunde."

"Tunde! How are you? What time is it over there?"

"It's about six."

"It is almost 2 AM here."

"Oh! I'm so sorry, ma! I will call back—"

"Nonsense. Is something wrong?"

"No. I just have a question to ask you."

"Does your daddy know that you are calling?"

"No."

"Do you know how expensive it is to call Nigeria?"

"Yes, ma."

"OK, ask me quickly so you won't get in trouble."

"OK. I'm just wondering how Mom is doing."

"What do you mean?"

"I mean, is she OK? Can she talk?"

"She is asleep right now."

"Can you wake her up?"

"No. She does not get much rest these days. Anytime that she falls asleep is a blessing."

"Is she doing better?"

"We thank God. Every day she is getting stronger."

"When can I talk with her?"

"I don't know. You should ask your father."

"OK."

"How is the weather over there?"

"It's really warm. It's been like ninety degrees all week."

"Ninety? Ah, ah! How is that possible?"

"That's actually normal for the summer."

"Ninety is normal? What are you saying? How are you still alive if ninety is normal?"

"It actually gets hotter by the middle of the summer."

"That isn't possible."

"Grandma, I'm serious! It gets really hot here."

"Ah, you have reminded me. In America you use crazy numbers for temperatures. What is the name of the system? Here it is centigrade."

"Oh. I just learned about that in school. We use Fahrenheit here."

"So what is ninety in centigrade?"

"I don't know."

"You must find out. I will ask you when we talk next, OK?"

"OK."

"Get off the phone before you get in trouble."

"Yes, ma."

"Greet your brother for me."

"Yes, ma."

"OK. Bye-bye."

"Bye."

A few weeks after the arrival of our new family members from Nigeria, my father called all of us into the living room and told us that he would be leaving his job at the Kodak plant in Salt Lake City. He asked us to sit on the couch and he sat down with us, and then he stood up and sat down again. With tears in his eyes, he told us that he had walked into his office, laughing with a coworker about something or other, and then he saw it: a crude drawing hanging by a red thread from the side of his cubicle. Someone had drawn a picture of my father with his facial features greatly exaggerated, and blood dripping from the extra-wide nose. The drawing was meant to be a representation of my father, an effigy, but he said the thing actually resembled an evil monkey.

Mom seemed shocked—her eyes grew large and she kept saying, "It can't be so. It can't be so." Femi rubbed Mom's back and Ade smiled like Dad had just announced that we were all going to Disney World. Tayo and I glanced at each other, and then Tayo stared down at the yellowing carpet. I could not help but shake my head. Though we were both scared, and angry, we weren't really surprised: We had heard different versions of this speech before. This was just the latest in a long series of job disappointments for him.

We knew that things had been easier for Dad once. At

other times, in other settings, Dad had regaled Tayo and me with stories about happier moments in his life. He would tell us how, as a young student in Nigeria almost fourteen years before, he had applied to a college in Utah on a whim, a school no one in his family had heard of, and how he'd learned shortly afterward that he'd been awarded a full scholarship. How his new school, Weber State University, had sponsored his trip to Utah, and covered the airfare for his new bride as well. How—unlike his siblings, his friends, almost everyone he knew—he had received a visa to travel to the United States on his first visit to the US Embassy in Lagos. How he felt hopeful even when he could not find a job in his chosen field, how he believed that his American dream would inevitably come true.

But then Mom got sick and left. Afterward Dad did all kinds of stuff—he worked as a mechanic, and then as a janitor at an amusement park, and then as a street sweeper, and then as a security guard. At first, each job seemed to present him with a host of possibilities, a chance to move up and make his mark, but then, inevitably, disappointment would follow. Sometimes he was laid off without explanation, and other times he quit because he was tired of being bullied. A threatening note left on his desk. An ugly word flung at his face.

Dad was always telling us that things would be getting better soon, but after a while we could tell that he had stopped believing this himself.

I still remember the day when Dad came home, so excited that it seemed like he was blushing, and told Tayo and me that he had been hired by Kodak. This was just a few months before our new mom and brothers arrived from Nigeria. Dad told us that the job didn't pay very much, but that he would get to wear a suit and tie every day. I remember being in awe of the idea that my father would actually have to dress up to go to work, instead of wearing one of the gray, drab jumpsuits that lined his musty closet. I helped Dad iron his favorite brown suit the night before his first day, the one with the missing top button and the small tear in the middle of the right sleeve. The next morning I felt so proud of him that I lingered in the car after he pulled up in front of my school, and I smiled at him like my face could do nothing else. Even though I'd spent my entire life in America, at that moment I felt as if we had all just arrived, and that everything was about to change.

After leaving Kodak, my father quickly found another job at a shop in Layton called Layton Rental. The place was filled with an assortment of machines that could be rented for varying periods of time. Dad seemed happy there, and he always answered the phone when I called:

"Hello, Layton Rental. Segun speaking!"

Sometimes I called just to hear his voice. He always sounded cheerful, even if he'd left home carrying sorrow in his eyes:

"Hello, Daddy! Can I have a lawn mower, please?"

"Yes, for how long?"

"I only need it for a couple minutes."

"Okay, that's fourteen million dollars."

"Daddy! I only have seven cents!"

"Okay, I will give you the Akinola discount. We will hold it for you. When are you coming?"

He often brought Tayo, Femi, and me to the shop, and I loved talking with Dad's coworkers as Dad worked the cash register, or showed a customer around. I also loved staring at the machines—lawn mowers, riding lawn mowers, chainsaws, all sputtering, oil-filled contraptions. They all seemed exotic at the time, even when my father turned a key or pulled a string or pressed a button to summon them to life. He always had a fun story for us after work, sometimes about an especially boorish customer, other times about a power drill he had repaired against all odds.

After a few months, though, my father began to come home angry. He told us he had decided that his accent was preventing him from getting ahead.

I had never heard him complain about his accent before. I didn't really know what an accent was. I knew Dad's voice was different—he didn't speak like my teachers or the social workers who occasionally stopped by our apartment to check up on Tayo and me after Mom returned to Nigeria—but in my mind the difference was a positive one. His voice sounded royal to me; I thought he had the kind of voice that everyone wanted, that through effort or fate, or perhaps a combination of both, he'd been blessed with a deep, forceful voice that instantly marked him as someone who was important.

Dad felt otherwise. At home he began to slam the phone down after repeating the same word four or five times to the person—always an American—on the other end. And then there was his charge to Tayo, Femi, and me as we sat around the dinner table one evening:

"Look here, you must have a perfect American accent,"

he said, calmly, icily. "People can say anything they want about the way you look, about your skin. But if you learn to speak better than them, there is *nothing* they can do. They cannot prevent you from moving ahead. Remember, everyone in this country is a racist. Even me. But if you learn to speak good, no one can hold you back."

At this Mom made a clucking noise. "Are you sure this is what you want to be telling your children?"

Tayo, Femi, and I began staring at our plates like they contained every dream we'd ever prayed for. Even Femi—who'd only been in America for a few weeks by then—knew better than to glance at Dad when he was being challenged. We knew that it was better for us to stare at the wall, our food, each other, to act as if we had no idea what was happening.

"What do you mean?" Dad growled.

"I mean, should you be teaching these children that everyone in America is a racist? Do you even believe that yourself?"

"Woman, I have been living in this country for more years than you have been working. I know what I am talking about. Why don't you keep quiet and bring me more food?"

Mom kept sitting, maybe for a second too long, but then she rose and picked up Dad's plate. Tayo, Femi, and I waited for a few beats, and then we stood as one and excused ourselves. We didn't hear a word from either of them for the rest of the night.

Dad began to make us watch the evening news so we'd learn how to speak what he called "professional English." I began to notice the differences.

My father said "chumorrow" and the white, well-coifed hosts said "tomorrow."

"Tomorrow, negotiations begin."

"Tomorrow, the president will meet with the grieving families."

"Tomorrow, the cease-fire goes into effect."

My father said "haboh" instead of "harbor." He said "biro" instead of "pen." He said "paloh" instead of "living room." My third-grade teacher asked me where my homework was, the day I forgot to bring it to school.

"I left it in my paloh, on the couch."

"Your *paloh*?"

I looked, confused, at my classmates, who tittered around me.

"My paloh. With the TV, couch, rug . . ."

My teacher smiled in recognition.

"Oh. You mean your *living room*. Okay, that's fine. Don't forget to bring it in tomorrow. And try to remember, when you're at school, it's a *living room*."

I burned with shame, then anger. Years later, I finally figured out that my father was saying "parlor."

Over time, I realized that an American would have to pass through two rooms before reaching my father's living room. First she would have to walk through a room of accent, a room brimming with thickets of syllables that were being twisted against their natural purpose. Then she would have to walk through a room crammed with old-world British terms. Weighty, abstracted words that my father had learned as a student in Nigeria in the 1950s, words that mean almost nothing in Britain today, and mean even less in America. And if she was patient enough to pass through both rooms, without even knowing what she was searching for, there was a chance she would happen upon the destination, the place my father had mentioned many moments before. Was it worth the effort? For some, yes. To others, though, my father didn't know what he was talking about. He was to be ignored.

My father became obsessed with the idea of starting his own business the moment my stepmother began working as a nurse at St. Benedict's Hospital—the biggest in town. She got the job about four months after she arrived, and Femi, Tayo, and I soon discovered (by huddling near our parents' bedroom door as they argued quite loudly one evening) that Mom's salary was substantially higher than Dad's. In the days following their argument my father began to complain even more about Layton Rental, about how his accent scared everyone because he sounded like the popular stereotype of the modern male African. I didn't know what a stereotype was, and when I asked him he told me to be quiet and go read my books.

Dad began to deliver rousing pep talks to himself at all hours of the day, even when he was driving us to school:

". . . that is the promise of this country! I must become an entrepreneur! That is my fate in this world! That is why God put me here! I am wasting my talents giving all my skill to these people! That's why I'm not getting ahead! I must take the horn by the bulls!"

He spoke this way for many weeks, but nothing really changed.

In January of '92, we moved from our apartment to a small brown house on Belnap Circle. It had three bedrooms and two bathrooms, and we actually had a garage, with an off-white garage door that clattered up or down after you flicked a switch inside. Tayo, Femi, and I took turns doing it whenever Mom and Dad were gone.

A few months later, in late spring, my father woke me up early on a rainy Saturday morning and told me we had somewhere special to go. He took me to the post office headquarters in Salt Lake City. We drove around the place until we saw the massive parking lot filled with dozens of gleaming white mail trucks; from afar they looked almost like large immobile sheep.

"My truck is there," he said, pointing toward the lot. "Trust me, Tunde, our lives will be changing very soon."

At the time I had no idea what he was talking about. When I asked him if he planned on becoming a mailman he smiled but he wouldn't answer. I thought his smile meant that I was right, and I tried to imagine him dropping letters off at the houses in our neighborhood instead of Mr. Peters, the kindly old man with the white, wispy mustache. I was suddenly scared for Mr. Peters because I didn't want him to lose his job because of my father.

Dad told us his plan a few days later, on the Friday before our last week of school, after waking my brothers and me up and asking us to gather in the paloh.

"Today, I am beginning my life again," he said. "I've quit my job at Layton Rental. I've purchased an old post office truck from the government. I will turn it into an ice cream truck. All of us will have to work together. Since you guys will be out of school in a few days, I expect that all of you will come with me when I start. We will have to work hard. If we honor what God has given us, God will honor us even more. Okay? Any questions?"

We shook our heads.

Dad smiled. He looked taller than usual, somehow, and his wide forehead was gleaming. A thin mustache sat delicately atop his upper lip.

"Okay! That's all."

The next morning, on Saturday, my father woke us up in his customary way. He stood in the doorway of our bedroom while the sun was still asleep and began to sing.

"Good morning, good morning, it's time to wake up! Good morning, good morning, it's time to wake up! Good morning, good morning, it's time to wake up! Doo doo doo! Doo doo doo! Doo doo doo!"

We groaned as loudly as we could when we heard the opening notes, but Dad simply sang over our complaints. The song had become a permanent fixture of our mornings by then, like deep yawns and bad breath. I didn't understand how someone could be so cheery in the morning. It was almost as if he were intentionally torturing us. When he finished singing Tayo, Femi, and I rolled out of our beds and quickly got ready in the bathroom, all of us in the shower at the same time. Then we dried ourselves, put on our clothes, and we stood in a line in the living room, as we did every Saturday morning. Dad emerged from his room a few moments later, and he paced up and down the line. Tayo and I stood straight and tall, but we giggled under our breath—we knew Dad was harmless, that he wouldn't punish us if it came to it. Femi stared ahead with a nervous expression, as if he were auditioning for the army. Right then I remembered how tense he'd seemed when I met him for the first time at the airport, and the way his eyes wouldn't stop moving, as if he'd expected more than he saw, or as if what he saw was more than he could comprehend.

"Are you guys ready?"

"Yes, sir!"

"What are we doing today?"

"Work, sir!"

"And how long will we work?"

"As long as it takes, sir!"

Satisfied, my father strode to the door and walked out, and we followed him. Outside, we saw an old postal truck and another car he hadn't told us about. Our ancient Chrysler station wagon was gone.

"Surprise!"

We rushed to the car. It was a light-blue Chevy sedan. The paint shimmered in the sunlight; the car looked brand-new. We danced around it, and Dad nodded.

"I bet you can't guess how much it was," he said, pointing at the car.

We laughed with incomprehension.

"Only five hundred dollars! The government gave me a discounted price because I bought it with the truck. Your daddy knows how to drive a bargain!"

But we were already inside the Chevy by then. I was doing

some great imaginary driving on an imaginary road, Tayo and Femi pointing out imaginary landmarks as we passed. Dad allowed us to play for a few minutes but then he called us back to the mail truck. He pointed to the truck and we gathered solemnly before it.

"This is our future," he said. "We must respect it."

We knew what he was actually saying; "respect" had mysteriously become a synonym for "clean like crazy" since our stepmother and stepbrothers had arrived from Nigeria. So we trudged into the garage and grabbed a few pails and sponges and followed Dad to the back of the truck. He turned a handle on the bottom of the back door and pushed the door up with both hands. Inside it looked much as I thought it would—big and empty and dirty—except for the steering column, which was positioned on the right-hand side of the truck. There were a few grimy shelves my brothers and I had to take apart and cart into the garage, and a couple registration stickers on the windshield that we couldn't remove despite our best efforts, but we had fun cleaning the floor and walls, occasionally blasting each other with the hose as Dad shouted directions outside. He inspected the truck when we finished, and after pointing out a few spots that we had supposedly missed, he called us into the Chevy. We drove for about fifteen minutes, past the houses of our neighborhood, then the shuttered neighborhood stores, with their broken windows and facades of peeling paint, and then past Wal-Mart and the colossal Sam's Club that had opened only a few weeks before. He parked in front of a large warehouse with a few trailers outside.

"Tunde, follow me inside. The rest of you, behave while we're gone."

A youngish-looking man with brown hair and porcelain skin smiled nervously as we walked in, and ushered us to a room in the back.

"I've been waiting for you guys! Glad you could finally make it . . ."

Dad ignored his unspoken question and the man shrugged and led us to an imposing door at the back of the room. He turned a wheel where a doorknob should have been and opened the door. The room exhaled frosty bursts of air all over us. We walked inside, shivering, and saw dozens of boxes piled atop each other. The man gestured to a pile of boxes off to one side.

"There's your order, sir. All the ice cream you asked for should be there."

My ears perked up. Ice cream?

"Thank you, sah."

Dad pointed to the boxes and I picked up a couple and carried them back to the car. "There's more inside," I told my brothers, and they tumbled out of the car to help. By the time we were finished we had filled the trunk and part of the backseat with boxes of ice cream. Dad jumped in and we sped back home. Once there, we carried the boxes to the freezer in the garage. It was an old 1960s-era freezer that made a great deal of noise, sometimes a hacking cough, other times a strangling sound, but it was very cold inside. We stacked the boxes neatly without opening them, and we called Dad when we were done.

"Good job," he said. Then he reached into the freezer and pulled a box from the middle. We gathered around him as he opened it, and we saw the tidy packages of ice cream stacked in perfect rows. Dad selected a package from the top, and we read the label aloud.

"Choco Taco," we said, in awed unison.

Dad smiled at us. Then he lifted the package to the ceiling and blessed it. He passed a package to each of us, and we sat down, in the middle of the garage, to consume our treats.

Tayo and I learned early on that all junkyards are basically the same. Dad had been taking us to junkyards all over Utah since we were toddlers, and we'd grown accustomed to the sights. At the front of the entire mess is a shack that's supposed to serve as an entryway, checkout counter, and, depending on the whims of the owner, a bar as well. Inside the shack there are car parts strewn all over the place: exhaust pipes on the counter, alternators and radiators spread across the floor, license plates everywhere. At the back of the shack there's a door that leads to the junkyard, a gate to another land.

For each junkyard is like an unexplored planet. The terrain is always unfamiliar; the air barely breathable. There are craters everywhere, and my father moves forward carefully, scouting the path ahead before calling back and telling us it's okay to follow. Every junkyard looks like the site of a massive industrial explosion, the secret innards of various contraptions laid out for us to see, while we roam about like postapocalyptic scavengers searching for the parts that will make our dying car go.

There wasn't much scavenging on this visit, though. Dad woke Tayo and me before dawn on the first day of our summer vacation and we drove to the Hartville Junkyard in our new ice cream truck. He asked the man behind the desk to follow us, and we walked through the industrial rubble until we came upon a long, sleek-looking freezer. Dad pointed at it.

"This is the one I want. How much?"

The man wheezed in response.

"For this? This is top of the line, yes, sir. This'll probably run you about . . . oh, I'd say about two-hundred fifty dollars."

"But it doesn't work," my father replied flatly.

"Don't matter. She's a looker. I could get someone to come out here and pay three hundred for her."

Back and forth they went until they settled on a price. One hundred eighty-five dollars, and the man threw in a carburetor for free. Dad laughed long and hard after the man left to draw up our receipt.

"See? What did I tell you? I drive the best bargains in all of Utah!"

We returned home with the freezer in the back of the truck, and Femi joined us in cleaning it. Femi still had a thick Nigerian accent then, and I couldn't decide if I liked him or not. This was the era when Tayo and I were basically the same person—same speech patterns (a solid middle-American accent spackled with the occasional Nigerian-accented phrase), same walk (a loping, confident gait that we'd adapted from our father's), and we each possessed a similar propensity for attracting occasional trouble (for various things, but we both excelled at watching television when there were dishes that needed washing). Femi's younger than Tayo and me, but he was our stepmother's oldest, and back then he carried himself like a kid with responsibility. I couldn't tell if he was acting perfect on purpose.

When we finished Dad told us to transfer a few boxes of ice cream from the freezer in the garage to the freezer in the truck. We did as we were told, and then Femi asked him how the ice cream would stay cold since the freezer didn't work. Dad turned around in his seat.

"Why don't you guys trust me? I have everything covered. Are you finished?"

We nodded and Dad immediately put the truck into reverse. We drove only a few minutes, to a small house across the street from Hartville High School. Yellow paint was peeling from the exterior, and the wooden steps leading up to the porch were cracked, but the house still had a solid, dependable aura about it.

"Femi and Tunde, follow me."

Dad knocked on the door and an older man with shoulder-length gray hair opened it. He was wearing a thin, plaid shirt and the top two buttons were undone. His gray chest hairs peeked out at us. Dad smiled and the man smiled back.

"You're . . ."

"Mr. Akinola," Dad said.

"Ah! Nice to meet you. So just one block, then?"

"Yes, sah."

"Okay, then, follow me."

"Can my children watch?"

"Of course they can. Come on down here, guys!"

We followed Dad and the old man to the basement. It was dim in there, but I could see a small freezer against the far wall, and an ancient-looking upright saw with rust on the blades resting beside it. The room was otherwise bare, save for a few movie posters on the wall. I didn't recognize any of the titles. The old man put on a pair of gloves that were resting on top of the freezer and pulled a steaming block of clouded ice from inside. He placed the ice on a tray that was attached to the saw and pressed a button at the base of it. Then he slid the ice back and forth before the screeching blade; solid slices separated themselves from the block until the block disappeared. The old man deftly wrapped each slice of clouded ice in brown paper, and he placed each slice in a large cardboard box.

"Here you go, sir," he said, handing the box over to Dad. "Remember what I said on the phone. This'll last you a couple days. Gotta treat it carefully. It'll burn you."

Dad turned to us.

"Are you listening to him? Did you hear what he said? I know you guys sometimes like to learn with your hands instead of your ears. If you don't listen, it will be a very painful lesson!"

I had no idea why we were being reprimanded in front of a man we'd never met before. In the truck Dad tore the paper off two of the packages and dropped the ice on the boxes in the freezer.

"What's that?" Femi asked.

"Dry ice," Dad said.

"But it will melt all over the ice cream, and the ice cream will get soggy," I said.

"No. It won't melt," Dad said. "It will only evaporate."

I thought he was playing a trick on us. When he turned away, I looked again at the ice in the freezer. Already the entire freezer was filling up with a thick fog. I pressed my finger to the mysterious ice, and a few seconds later I felt a stinging fire flow from the tip of my finger to the top of my arm.

I screamed. Dad whirled around and caught me with my finger on the ice. I couldn't pull it away. He quickly opened a bottle of water that was near the gearshift and poured it over the ice until my finger came loose. I looked at my quivering finger and noticed that my skin had burned away, leaving only a red pulsating sketch of the skin that had once been there.

"What did I tell you about touching that ice, Tunde? What did I tell you?"

I hung my head in shame and Dad started laughing, booming his voice in my direction. I knew what was coming next.

"GOOOOOOOOD FOR YOOOOOOOOU!"

My brothers laughed along with him.

Dad put the rest of the dry ice into the old freezer in the garage when we got home. Then he went inside and emerged a few moments later with a small cardboard box.

"The final step," he said.

He opened the box and pulled out a rectangular device that had two switches on the top and a mess of wires on the bottom. I couldn't read what was written beneath the switches because Dad took the device inside the truck and started working. We saw him battling with wires and pliers; we heard him curse occasionally under his breath. We eventually grew tired of watching him and went inside to watch TV. Dad strolled into the living room an hour later and told us to come outside. He went in on the driver's side of the truck and clicked something, and we heard a familiar song flowing out of the horn-shaped speaker he'd placed at the front of the truck, just above the windshield.

"That's the ice cream music!" Tayo cried. We recognized the tune from the ice cream trucks we'd seen on TV. We'd never seen an ice cream truck in Hartville, though.

Dad nodded excitedly. Then we linked arms and listened together.

The following morning Dad woke us up with his good-morning song, and when we reached the garage we saw an old, thin, beat-up mattress on the floor.

"Put it in the back of the truck," he said. "That's where you guys will relax between your shifts."

We placed the mattress where he told us, right up against the freezer, and we brought along a couple pillows so the bed would be even more comfortable. As we were reclining on it Dad appeared and stared at us.

"Aren't you forgetting something?"

Tayo, Femi, and I looked at each other, and then we looked around. Dad shook his head slowly.

"What about your books? What do you think this is?

A time to rest? If you aren't working then you're reading! Go bring your books!"

We ran back inside and brought out a couple of books and placed them on the mattress. Dad surveyed the titles and shook his head again.

"Bring more. I expect each of you to finish one book each day."

We brought more books and piled them high against the freezer. Dad nodded, then he settled in the driver's seat and started the engine. He flipped on the music and began to back out, but then Mom stepped into the garage and called him. Dad switched off the engine and left the truck.

We stared out of the windshield as Dad approached Mom. They stood looking at each other for a moment. Mom said something. Dad shook his head and stared at the garage floor. Mom said something else. Dad threw his hands in the air and stepped back. Mom looked up at the ceiling. They just stood there. Then Mom stepped forward and hugged Dad. After standing there with his arms at his sides for a few moments, Dad hugged her back.

Dad returned to the truck with a smile on his face, and Mom went back inside and closed the door. Dad began humming to himself as he turned the ignition. He drove down the length of our street, took a right onto Jones Place, and then he slowed down. We knew better than to ask Dad what he and Mom had discussed, so we tried to ask him with our eyes. He continued humming as if he couldn't see us, so we stared out of the windows instead as we crawled down one street after another.

Tayo, Femi, and I were familiar with these streets; we'd spent hours walking around our neighborhood in search of kids our age or older who might be interested in playing basketball with us, but our neighborhood looked different, somehow, from the windows of our ice cream truck. The houses looked the same, like precise replicas of our own house, with their small front lawns and brown-tiled roofs, but now the people we saw walking their dogs and kicking soccer balls were no longer friends, or even neighbors—they were all potential customers. A few people simply stared at our truck as we passed, but from the way they looked we might as well have been foreigners engaged in an inspection tour of newly conquered territory, or a single-car parade drifting by. Most of the people we saw ignored us completely. On two occasions we saw a child looking expectantly in our direction and we yelled at Dad to stop. Dad listened and pulled the truck over to the curb, but both times the child shyly waved at us and ran away. We continued searching for customers, but after we'd been on the road for an hour or so my brothers settled down in the back to read. Dad asked me to sit on the chair he'd placed in front of the freezer, right behind his chair. I sat there reading while Dad hummed along with the music.

A few moments later the truck jarred to a stop. I rose from my seat and looked out the driver's side window. There was a young man with short blond hair and pimply skin standing on the sidewalk, holding a small child to his chest. When Dad extended his hand the man pulled his child away, but Dad kept his hand in the air and smiled at him. I'd never seen this particular smile on my father's face before. It was so kind, without a trace of malice or hurt or sarcasm or shame. The man looked at Dad's extended hand, and then at Dad's smile, and he slowly pushed his child's body in the direction of Dad's hand. Dad stroked the child's head.

The man laughed nervously. "It's sure nice to see you here. Certainly hot enough for ice cream. How much do you charge?"

Dad started, and then he turned to his right to peer at the stickers we'd affixed to the side of the truck the night before. The stickers featured artistic renderings of the ice cream bars we'd stacked in our freezer beneath islands of dry ice. As Dad stared at the stickers, I realized that we'd neglected to indicate how much each kind of ice cream would cost.

"Well, since you're our first sale, tell me what you want and how much you want to pay for it," Dad said confidently.

The man scrunched up his face and shook his head. "What did you say?"

Dad enunciated: "Choose something and pay what you want."

The man whispered into the ear of his child and leaned forward slightly so the child could whisper back. He whispered again, listened, then looked up.

"How about a Creamsicle for a dollar?"

Dad motioned to me and I opened the freezer and reached into the upper left corner, where I'd carefully placed a box of Creamsicles the night before. I pulled one free from the pack and handed it to Dad. Dad handed the bar to the child, who wrapped its little fingers around it and smiled at us in appreciation.

"Don't worry about paying. I hope to see you soon."

When they left I grabbed the permanent marker from the desk at the front of the truck and waved it near Dad's face.

"Daddy, we need to mark the prices on the stickers!"

"No, let's wait. Let's see what happens."

My father continued to drive around the city without any plan. Sometimes we passed down the same street twice, and whenever someone called to us we'd stop and let them decide the price. Dad spoke in short, declarative sentences, and he asked me to speak if our customers had more questions. We gave some ice cream away, and we sold some for a couple dollars apiece. As darkness came on we drove back home a few dollars richer.

Tayo, Femi, and I were already out of the truck when Dad reminded us that we had to move the boxes of ice cream from the dead freezer in the truck to the grunting freezer in the garage. We quickly emptied the freezer in the truck and when we saw the mess inside the freezer in the garage we called Dad. He ran to us, and when he saw it he stepped back and cursed loudly.

The freezer was lukewarm and the ice on the sides had melted. A congealed multicolored mass of melted ice cream had pooled on the bottom. The freezer had failed.

Dad stood staring at the ground and we waited because we didn't know what we were supposed to do. He turned around and began walking back to the truck.

"Help me put all the ice cream back into the truck," he called.

We did as we were told, and just as we were finishing

Mom came out of the house. She was wearing a thin blue wrapper and paint-splotched flip-flops. She rubbed her arms and stared at each of us before her eyes settled on Dad. "What's wrong?" she said. "Why aren't you guys excited? How was your first day?" Dad shook his head and stepped into the truck. He started up the engine.

"Tunde, follow me."

I bounded into the truck and stared at Mom as we pulled away. Her face was blank and her smile was dimming, dimming, fading like a dying lightbulb.

My brothers and I felt Dad's heat when he entered our bedroom the following morning, so we woke up before he could shout at us. We dressed quickly and ran to the truck. I opened the freezer and saw the evaporating islands of dry ice atop the boxes. I pressed the packages of ice cream with my index finger; they felt firm and cold. We were already prepared— sitting in the back of the truck, reading studiously—by the time Dad climbed into the driver's seat. He looked back at us without saying a word, and then he started the engine.

"Daddy, what about the prices?" I asked, tentatively.

Dad switched off the ignition and left the truck with the permanent marker. I went out with him and he looked down at me.

"So what should we do?"

I'd been thinking about it all night and I'd prepared an answer:

"Why don't we make everything fifty cents?"

Dad smiled for the first time.

"Do you know how much each ice cream cost me? And I have to pay for gas, dry ice, and make enough for us to eat."

"Okay, how about fifty-five cents?"

Dad laughed.

"Who are you trying to help? Your family? Or the strangers who will be buying from us? You must learn that there are times to be nice, and there are times to be mean." With that Dad handed me the marker, and he called out the prices as I pointed to each of the stickers. I copied down the prices in neat blocky script.

Our second day on the road was quite different from our first. Dad drove with purpose this time, and we passed by more schools and playgrounds. He didn't laugh with us as he had the day before; he kept his eyes on the side of the road, searching for anyone with even the smallest quantity of desire in their eyes. Our first sale came much more quickly. After about ten minutes on the road we were flagged down by three teenagers on a playground.

"Hey, man! We didn't know anyone sold ice cream around here! Whaddya got?"

Dad pointed to the side of the truck.

"Pick whatever you like, I have a full freezer today, gentlemen."

I peered at each of them, hoping I'd recognize a friend, or at least an acquaintance. I wanted, desperately, to meet someone I knew, someone who would return to school and tell everyone that my father sold ice cream. I knew it was my only chance at the kind of popularity I'd coveted my entire life. Once word got out, people would want to know more about my father, more about my family and—most important—more about me. I had all my answers ready.

(I stopped caring by the middle of the summer. Whenever I saw anybody I knew I could tell from the way they looked at me that they still thought I was a loser. I mean, who was I trying to kid? My parents were still from Africa, I still had a weird name, and we still weren't Mormons. A little ice cream selling wasn't going to change any of that.)

We stayed on the road past sundown, and by the time we pulled onto our street Femi was sleeping on the bed in the back, and I'd already exchanged places with Tayo at least twice. When I opened the freezer I noticed that it was half-empty, and our makeshift cash register at the front of the truck was filled with one-dollar bills. Dad rubbed his eyes after parking, and he cleared his throat the way he always did when he had an announcement.

"We did okay today, guys. We'll do better tomorrow."

Then he stepped out of the van, pulled on some gloves, and packed more dry ice into the freezer.

By the end of our first week on the road we had developed a system. Dad insisted that I accompany him each day while Tayo and Femi rotated during weekdays (someone had to stay home and look after Ade). Mom would rise before us each day to prepare our meals for the road, which she placed in used Styrofoam packaging that had formerly held Chinese food or hamburgers. At midday Dad would stop at a parking lot somewhere and we would swallow our cold fufu or jollof rice or fried plantain, and then we'd start out again.

We did better as it got hotter. By the middle of the summer, as word spread about our ice cream truck, we'd drive onto certain streets where hungry crowds had already gathered. Tayo, Femi, or I would hustle at the freezer while the kids and adults called out their orders. Some days we woke up well before dawn to buy more ice cream from the wholesalers downtown.

Occasionally on the road Dad would tell us stories about Nigeria. He made the place sound like a wonderful party that was always happening. He told us stories about each of his brothers—he has dozens; my grandfather married six women—and he wistfully spoke of the time he'd spent traveling from city to city as a semiprofessional soccer player. He also told us stories about the mistakes he'd made as a younger man; the women he'd chased just because he could, the jobs he hadn't taken seriously enough. Each story he told ended abruptly, or at least it seemed so to me. I was always waiting to hear about the day his apartment had been stormed by corrupt policemen, the time he'd been incarcerated for something he hadn't done. I was waiting to hear that he was a refugee—back then I thought this was the only legitimate reason for leaving a place you called home. I knew nothing about ambition then, how it wakes you up and won't let you sleep at night, how it'll fling you across an ocean or three if you let it. I would learn soon enough.

As I look back on those days now I often think of all the fun that Tayo, Femi, and I had in the back of the truck, the way we would pull out a deck of cards whenever Dad was occupied with a sale and toss the cards under a pillow the moment he was done; and also our fights, our screaming and clawing and shoving and snarling; the way Dad would shout at us; all of us angry with him at the same time; the secrets we shared with one another; the stories we made up about our favorite customers; the many silent hours of reading and contemplation; the deep, sunny stillness of those late afternoons when the sun was drifting toward the western horizon and all of us were drunk on happiness and light.

The only unpleasant aspect of all those mornings, afternoons, and late evenings on the road was the fact that Dad didn't allow us to eat as much ice cream as we would have liked. Initially, of course, we'd been excited about Dad's ice cream business because we'd envisioned a future in which we did nothing but gorge ourselves on sumptuous cream-filled treats. Dad thought differently. He rarely allowed us to eat more than one ice cream bar a day, and he was hesitant to allow us to eat any ice cream that was in perfect condition.

After we'd been on the road for a week or so, Dad drafted an "ice cream consumption hierarchy chart" and pasted it to the wall just behind the freezer. On the bottom of the paper he'd written, in all caps, BAD ICE CREAM. By this he meant ice cream that was ill-formed or otherwise imperfect because of some manufacturing defect; sometimes an errant stick, sometimes a crumbled cone. Above, he'd written MELTED ICE CREAM. This was the ice cream that had melted during transport and had refrozen in odd, unsellable shapes. And then there was the CHEAP ICE CREAM—the Fudgsicles and Creamsicles for example. Above the cheap ice cream was the OK ICE CREAM—ice cream sandwiches and premium ice pops—and shining above everything else was the SUPREME ICE CREAM (he drew a circle of stars around the word "supreme"); the aforementioned Choco Taco, the large ice cream sandwiches, the super-deluxe ice cream cones. Dad expected us to start at the bottom of the chart when we were selecting our ice cream for the day, and so on most days the best we could hope for was an "OK" ice cream; usually, though, my brothers and I would chomp on our bad or melted ice cream bars with frowns on our faces to emphasize to Dad how unhappy we were. He never seemed to notice.

Dad tried very hard to sell each of the supreme ice cream bars, even the bad and melted ones. He'd brandish them about after completing a large sale—"Are you sure you guys don't want any more? I am selling these at half price!"—and he usually ended up selling most of them. If, at the end, a few of these melted masterpieces went unsold, he would grudgingly allow us to eat them, but only if there were enough for each of us. Otherwise we'd take them home, and he and Mom would divvy up the bounty.

My brothers and I came up with a few tricks to increase our chances of eating those supreme ice cream bars. Sometimes we'd forget to place the dry ice on the parts of the freezer that held the most expensive ice cream, and they would melt as a result. We'd present the spoiled goods to my father with sad eyes and sad tales to match:

"I don't know what's wrong, Daddy. The ice doesn't seem to be working. Maybe we need to get something that's stronger?"

Dad soon caught on, so we tried other tricks. We'd slam the expensive boxes of ice cream on the hard floor of the freezer while we were packing the truck, in hopes that a few of the precious bars would break. We'd bang the ice cream against the side of the freezer during an especially hectic sale and present it to Dad. He'd return the bars to us—"This one is broken"—and we'd smilingly place the ice cream in the empty box near the back of the freezer that we reserved for spoiled ice cream.

Dad caught on to these tricks as well, but he never became upset. Usually our plans failed because we were rarely able to produce the four spoiled ice cream bars that we needed in order to be successful. As the summer passed, Dad's stomach became bigger for our failures.

Sometime during the middle of summer, maybe late July or early August, one of our regular customers—he lived three streets down from us, quite near my elementary school—suggested that we park our truck on Main Street during the annual Hartville City Fair.

"You'll make a killing!" the man said, smiling as ice cream dripped from his buckteeth. "There's never any ice cream around—you should jump on it before someone else gets the same idea!"

Dad asked for more information and the man told him everything—that the fair took place on the Friday and Saturday of Labor Day weekend, just before school started; how the fairgrounds extended all the way down Main Street, right through the middle of town; how there were kiosks for everything: cotton candy, caramel apples, and popcorn; how there were games and a few rides; how there were even a few people who sold snow cones from small coolers, but no ice cream trucks. We'd never heard of the fair even though we'd been living in Hartville for over a year by then, and as the man described one spectacle after another I wondered how something so wonderful had escaped our attention for so long. We were partly to blame, I knew—we mostly stayed to ourselves. We hadn't really traveled much around the city, and my parents didn't have any friends. Our house was a miniature Nigeria, with its own customs and culture, and I didn't know much about the world outside. I interpreted our ignorance of the Hartville City Fair as just another sign that we would never truly fit in Utah, that the various mysteries of the place would forever remain closed to us, because we weren't Mormon, because we were black.

Dad suddenly became infatuated with the fair, and for the rest of the day he spoke of nothing else. He talked himself into the idea that the Hartville City Fair was the reason he'd started selling ice cream in the first place, that God's will had been revealed to him through the words of one of his favorite customers. By the time we returned home that evening the Hartville City Fair had become something we'd been waiting for all our lives. Dad went to City Hall first thing the following morning and applied for a vendor's license. He returned disappointed; he told us that they'd asked him to fill out a few forms, that they'd said they would contact him in a few days. We didn't hear anything from them in the following weeks, though, despite the fact that Dad pestered them continually. He even drafted Tayo and me to the cause of calling the city council to plead our case. "These people always respond better to an American accent," he said. So he called, and we called, we even assumed bland American names and bland American accents on the phone, but we garnered no response.

Meanwhile, our ice cream business was going so well that Dad decided to purchase another US Postal Service truck. He left with Mom early one morning in August for Salt Lake City and they both returned driving trucks, Dad behind the wheel of our ice cream truck, and Mom driving a retired mail truck. We quickly converted the mail truck into an ice cream truck; we scrubbed the inside and outside, removed the various shelves and boxes that had once held countless letters, removed the red and blue stripes from the exterior, and we placed stickers featuring perfect versions of the imperfect ice cream that we sold each day on both sides of the truck. After we finished Dad told us to help him pull the dead freezer out of our first truck and into the garage, and then he drove off again. He beeped loudly when he returned, and we saw a U-Haul trailer attached to the truck. We opened the trailer to a new freezer, and as we laughed Dad said, "And this one works!" He opened the back of the truck to reveal another new freezer.

We helped Dad carry the new freezer out of the trailer and into the new truck, and then we went inside to rest. Dad came into the living room shortly afterward and asked us what we were doing. He'd already changed into his customary ice cream selling outfit—a loose-fitting dark-blue short-sleeve dress shirt and dark-blue slacks. Femi and I ran outside and hopped into our first truck as Dad was starting it, and we went off for a half day of selling.

Dad spent a week trying to find someone to drive the second truck. He placed an ad in the paper and a few people stopped by our house quite early in the morning, before we started our day, and a few came late at night, after we'd come back. He finally settled on a twenty-four-year-old named Jerry whom he liked because Jerry had referred to him as "sir." Jerry claimed he was trying to save enough money to return to college, and Dad liked that story, too. Tayo and I didn't tell Dad about the time we caught Jerry smoking in the backyard while he was waiting for Dad to return from the wholesale ice cream warehouse with ice cream for his truck.

To this day I don't know what kind of arrangement my father worked out with Jerry regarding the sharing of revenue, but after only a week of working together Jerry simply stopped showing up. When Tayo asked Dad at dinner what had happened, he told us not to worry. "I will find someone better," he said.

Dad eventually found someone else to drive the second ice cream truck, and then someone else when that person quit, and then someone after that. They all eventually left because Dad drove them too hard and because he demanded a quota of ice cream sold each day.

Dad began to push himself harder as well. He woke up at four in the morning every day so he could peer at the big map of Hartville he'd purchased a couple weeks into summer. Sometimes he'd wake me up as well, and I would try to keep my eyes open as he traced new paths of ice cream dominance in red ink on the map. He'd bite the tip of his pen while concentrating on a particular quadrant of the map, mumbling incoherently to himself, scribbling red lines next to other red lines, crossing out some routes completely, like he was planning his takeover of the city. When he was done he'd leave the map on the table for one of us to fold up, and he'd walk whistling out the door, his new route inscribed in his brain. We drove for longer hours each day, and Dad became adept at ingratiating himself with every person he met on the road. I'd never known him to be such a flirt, such a politician. If he saw an old woman crossing the street he'd lower the music and speak coolly to her, his voice like a blast of cold air from an oscillating fan:

"Madame! You look so lovely! How are you this afternoon? Can I interest you in a Creamsicle to help ease you on your way?'

And even if she rejected his advances, even if she ignored him completely, Dad would continue smiling.

"Well, God bless you! And I expect you to buy something the next time I see you!"

At night, after I put on my pajamas and before I fell asleep, Dad would ask me to sit next to him at the kitchen table, and together we would read passages from my favorite books. I would read a few paragraphs and then Dad would repeat them, mimicking my tone, my accent, the way my lips wrapped themselves around each word. As I fell asleep each night I'd hear my father's voice in my head narrating passages from books by Isaac Asimov, Ray Bradbury, J. R. R. Tolkien, and Ursula K. Le Guin. Over time, he began to sound like me.

August suddenly became September. We were stopped more often as we drove down the streets of Hartville, and the crowds that gathered to meet us at our high-traffic areas grew larger. But the entire time I couldn't stop thinking about the fair. I wondered if we'd be able to sell ice cream there. I wondered how our lives would change if they allowed us to participate; if, at the end, I would finally understand what it meant to be a part of a community.

We finally heard from the city council a few days before the fair, and it was good news. Dad immediately went to the ice cream wholesalers and placed his largest order of the summer.

"Business must be going well," the man said as he handed over box after box of ice cream.

"You have no idea," Dad said as he handed the boxes to me. "I might be putting you out of business soon."

They both laughed too loudly.

On the first day of the fair we all woke up at 4 AM and began to make preparations. Mom brewed two big pots of stew and pulled the moin moin she'd prepared the night before from the fridge. While she fried up some plantains the rest of us packed each freezer as full of ice cream as we could, and Dad and Freddy—Dad had hired him the day before; he looked just like Jerry, maybe shorter, maybe younger, but basically the same—left with both trucks to buy dry ice. When they returned we stashed the food in the back of the trucks and stepped in so Dad and Freddy could drive us to Main Street. Mom and Ade followed in our Chevy.

When we arrived we saw other vendors preparing for the day and policemen going from stand to stand, asking to see vendor passes. The policemen came to our trucks and Dad proudly showed them ours. They nodded and continued on. Dad asked us to gather in a circle and hold hands. We prayed together under the rising sun.

"God, we thank you for your blessings. We thank you that we are the first ice cream vendors who have been allowed to participate in this festival, O Lord. We didn't know about this festival before now, but we thank you that we learned in time, and that we were blessed with an opportunity to be here. God, please bless us today, so that the line of people who ask us for ice cream will not stop. We want them to continue to come and ask for ice cream as if they have never tasted ice cream in their lives. God, you have finally given us an opportunity to make it in this country. This is our chance. Help us to make the most of it."

We said a loud "amen" together, and my father became a different person. He peeled off his smile.

He pointed at Freddy. "Go and park where I told you to park last night. Stay there. Tayo will go with you. If anything happens, send him down to this truck with a message. Do not mess around today. I am not playing with you. This is the day that can make the rest of our lives."

Freddy slinked away, scowling, and Tayo and Ade followed him. Dad turned to the rest of us.

"I chose this part of the street for a reason. According to my sources in city hall, the busiest part of the festival will be here. That means we'll be working nonstop. Mom already knows that she'll have to go back home if we need more food, or if we need more ice cream. Tunde, Femi, I need everything you have today. You cannot let up. Keep moving forward, no matter what."

We both nodded.

We sat in the truck and waited as the sun continued its upward path. The chaos around our truck began slowly. Outside, jugglers threw bright balls into the air, and loud music began pumping from large speakers on either side of us. The music was so loud that I could almost see the musical notes curling up out of the speakers. A man came walking by with a card deck and he flashed a few cards at Femi and me as we peered out of the driver's side window. Our eyes flashed in response, but we felt Dad's hard gaze knocking on our backs, so we turned away from him.

People of all kinds began to walk around, and a few of them stopped by our truck. I stood ready at the freezer and passed Dad the ice cream they were asking for before their tongues had formed the second syllable, so practiced was I. As the day grew hotter more people stopped by, and soon a line snaked around our truck and down the length of the street for many feet. Femi and I worked together, huffing and puffing into the freezer, developing a rhythm of delivery while Dad worked complex figures in his head and passed the ice cream to our customers. By eleven we were on the verge of running out of a few items, and Dad sent me to the other truck to see if we could get any more supplies from them.

I saw the long line as I approached the other truck, and I had to apologize many times because a few people thought I was trying to cut in front of them. I knocked on the back of the truck and Tayo opened it for me, and then he rushed back to Freddy with a package of ice cream in his hand. Ade was playing with a ball on the bed, and he giggled at me when I waved. I asked Tayo if they had any extra boxes of snow cones or Fudgsicles, and he shook his head.

I sprinted back and told Dad the news, and he dispatched Mom to the house to pick up more ice cream. We were already out of a few items by the time she returned, and a great cheer rose up as she walked through the crowd, carrying boxes of ice cream above her head.

I placed my hand on my father's shoulder and he turned around and smiled at me. His smile was wide and wondrous. Suddenly I wanted to hug him and tell him it would always be like this. I wanted to tell him that he would always be a star. I wanted to live in this moment for the rest of my life, to forget what I had seen while I was out trying to get more ice cream for the truck.

Just before I reached Freddy's truck, I noticed a few men standing in a circle a few feet down the street. One of them was licking a Firecracker Popsicle. The Firecracker looked delicious; its red-white-and-blue segments sparkled in the sun. The man pulled the Firecracker from his mouth and oinked loudly, and then he began to speak in a melodramatic, garbled manner. Spittle flew from his lips. I couldn't make out what he was saying. In the midst of his performance I heard him say "Creamsicle"; the other men laughed and slapped their thighs. That's when I realized they were making fun of my father. I ignored them and kept walking.

I already knew that the weather was growing colder and my brothers and I would soon be returning to school. I knew that in a few days my father would park his trucks for the winter, that the moment he did so he would just be an immigrant again.

But I also knew that my father was content. I knew he was calm and proud. I knew that—for the first time in a long time—he was in control. He had achieved everything he set out to achieve.

And besides—our day was just beginning. We had more ice cream to sell. And the weather was perfect. I knew we were going to sell more ice cream than we'd ever sold before.

Tomorrow was coming, but I was happy. My father still had a few hours left in the sun.

GRANDMA + TUNDE

"*Tunde, come get the phone!*"

I ran into the kitchen and Dad passed the phone to me. "*It's your grandma,*" he said gruffly. Then he paused and stared at the fridge. "*The only thing these people care about is money. They must think that I'm made of money. They must think that I don't do anything but sit on my ass and count money all day long.*" He shook his head and walked away. A few moments later I heard a door slam.

"*Hello?*"

"*Hello, Tunde? Is that you?*"

"*Yes, ma.*"

"*How are you today?*"

"*I'm fine, ma.*"

"*That's good. Is your father still there?*"

"*No*"

"*OK.*"

"*What happened?*"

"*Don't you worry about it.*"

"*You can tell me.*"

"*It is not for your ears. If your father wants to tell you, then he will tell you.*"

"*OK.*"

"*Tunde, are you still there?*"

"Yes."

"OK, sorry, I couldn't hear you. One of your cousins is here. Do you want to speak with her?

"Who?"

"It's Shola. Do you remember her? You've spoken with her on the phone a few times. Especially when you were younger."

"I don't remember her."

"OK, you will remember when you speak with her. Here she is."

"Hello? Hello?"

"Hello."

"Can you hear me?"

"Yes."

"Is this Tunde?"

"Yes."

"Tunde! How are you?"

"I'm doing OK."

"How old are you now?"

"I'm ten."

"Ten! Wow, you are growing up fast!"

"I guess."

"Do you remember me?"

"I'm sorry, but I don't."

"Oh, that's OK. When are you coming to Nigeria?"

"I don't know."

"You have to come soon! Don't forget us, oooo. Don't forget that you are a Nigerian! You will always be a Nigerian!"

"OK."

"How are your studies?"

"I'm doing fine."

"That's good. I myself am getting ready for university. I have applied to a school in the US, maybe you have heard of it. Williams College."

"I haven't heard of it."

"OK. I am coming to visit the US soon, if your father can help me. That's what Grandma was talking to him about. Maybe I can come and visit you. You are still in Utah, right?"

"Yes."

"How do you like it over there?"

"It's OK, I guess."

"OK. My mother wants to speak with you. Hold on."

"Hello, Tunde?"

"Hello, ma."

"How are you?"

"I'm fine, ma."

"I can't stay on the phone for long, I just wanted to check on you. I haven't spoken with you in five years! Why don't you call us?"

"I can't because it is too expensive to call Nigeria."

"All of you with the same excuse. All of you leave Nigeria because you want to get more money, and then when you get to the US you are always complaining that you have no money. Why don't you come back, then? Why stay poor in a place so far from home? It is better to be poor at home."

"I'm sorry, ma."

"Tunde, I'm sorry. I am just frustrated with . . . with certain things."

"It's OK."

"How old are you now, Tunde?"

"I'm ten."

"OK, describe yourself for me."

"What do you mean?"

"I don't know how you look, so describe yourself. How do you look?"

"Ummm . . ."

"Do you look like your father or mother?"

"I don't remember how my mother looks. But I think I look my dad. Maybe a smaller version of him."

"Do you have his nose? That wide nose of his?"

"Yes."

"Why do you sound sad?"

"Because I hate my nose. I've always hated it."

"Hate, ke! How can you hate something that God has given you?"

"Because it's too big."

"It's not too big, oh. That is the other problem with that country. Everyone will be telling you that your nose is too big because you don't have that small-small white-man nose. That nose that they are struggling to breathe with. Don't mind them! Your nose is beautiful. Ask your father how many women were stroking his nose when he was a young man."

"OK."

"Ok-o, I have to go. Tell your father that he must call more often. And tell him to help us if he can."

"OK."

"OK, bye!"

"Bye!"

"Tunde! Tunde? Are you still there?"

"Yes, Grandma. I am here."

"How is your mother?"

"I don't know. She's over there."

"I mean your new mom. Your mom over there. How is she?"

"She's fine, I guess."

"How are both of you getting along?"

"We're fine."

"You don't sound fine."

"I'm fine, ma."

"What is wrong, now?"

"Nothing, ma."

"Are you fighting with her?"

"No, ma."

"Are you treating her well?"

"Yes, ma."

"Is she treating you well?"

"Yes."

"OK. Good boy. Don't you realize what a blessing you have? You have two moms! Most people only have one."

"Yes, ma."

"Don't forget that. There are two women in this world who love you dearly, who love you as only a mother can. Try to remember that."

"Yes, ma."

"OK, give the phone to Tayo."

"How is Mom? I mean, my mom over there?"

"She is fine. She is resting. I will tell her you said hello."

"When can I talk to her?"

"Not now. She isn't here."

"Where is she?"

"She is at church. Don't worry. You will talk to her soon."

"Yes, ma."

"OK, give the phone to your brother and remember to be a good boy. And tell your father to call me more often!"

"Yes, ma."

"Tunde? Are you still there?"

"I'm here, ma."

"There's something else I want to tell you. About your mother. Your new mother."

"OK."

"There comes a time in life when you can no longer focus on what others are doing to you, but on the life you are living. You are a young man now, so you must focus on yourself. Do you understand?

"Yes, ma."

"Even though both of your mothers love you very much, you can't depend on them or anyone else to take care of your heart. You have to learn how to do this yourself. That is part of being an adult."

"Yes, ma."

"So I want you to focus on you. On the things that make you happy and calm. The things that make your heart beat faster and slower. This is how you will learn who you are, and what you are supposed to do in this life."

"Yes, ma."

"OK, let me talk to Tayo."

I called Tayo and placed the phone on the counter. Then I went to the bathroom and closed the door.

I couldn't stop staring at him. The nerdy-looking kid in the mirror. Was he a young man? He didn't seem like a man to me. Just young. I repeated my grandmother's words. "You are a young man now," I said to the mirror. He seemed to be talking back.

"You are a young man now. You must focus on yourself."

I smiled. I felt different. Better.

I kept saying those words.

November 7, 2000
6:41 AM

I think something is wrong with me.

I'm not sure how to describe it. It has something to do with my imagination. The way things live in my mind.

I've always had an active imagination. For example, I believed in Santa Claus long after my siblings and friends did. Right up until I was in middle school. Whenever Santa failed to show up—every year he failed to show up—I always blamed myself. I thought about everything I'd said or done over the course of the year, and I always remembered some time that I'd disobeyed my father, some time I'd been envious or unappreciative or, as I grew older, some time that I'd glanced at a girl and wondered how she looked without her clothes. I always resolved to do better the following year, and then, inevitably, I'd mess up somehow, and I'd hope that Santa wasn't watching, that somehow he'd missed it. And when Christmas came and there were no presents under our plastic misshapen tree I'd shake my head and feel guilty and frustrated with myself. I don't think there was a moment when I decided I didn't believe in Santa. I just grew to accept disappointment as an inevitable part of my life.

I also believed that professional wrestling was real until, well, very recently. I was always upset whenever the sportscaster on the local news failed to discuss the results of WrestleMania or SummerSlam. My parents never had enough money to purchase those pay-per-views, so I'd have to wait until Monday when some rich kid would tell the rest of us what had happened, and I'd envision the matches in my head, everything appearing as clearly as it would on any screen. Eventually the kids at school stopped caring about wrestling. This did not matter to me. I kept watching those matches in my head.

I also imagined the things I wanted in the future. Impossible things, things that could never happen to a poor black kid like me. But at night I'd close my eyes and see myself graduating at the top of my class in high school. I'd see myself dating a woman who looked just like Lauryn Hill. I'd see myself in Nigeria, talking with my mother as if we had never been apart. And I'd see myself getting a full ride to Morehouse College, the school I learned about when my brother and I were living at the homeless shelter with Mom, the school Martin Luther King Jr. had graduated from. The school made up entirely of smart black men. The school where I would no longer be unusual. I saw each of these things so clearly that I had no doubt whatsoever that they would all come true.

Well, some of them came true. A few months ago I graduated at the top of my high school class, and I'm typing this from my dorm room at Morehouse College.

Recently, though, I've begun to see other things. I see things I could have done as if I have done them. Just a few days ago, for example, my roommate Maceo invited me to a party at his girlfriend's house. She's a junior and lives off campus, and every now and then she'll invite a few people over for games and drinks and stuff, and every time Maceo comes back he'll tell me how incredible it was, about all the fine girls who were there. He's always telling me that I'm missing out, and I was so tempted to go with him this last time, but I had a big test I needed to study for, so I decided to do that instead. When I saw him the next morning Maceo told me how much fun he'd had, and I still don't know how this is even possible but I suddenly remembered being there. I remembered feeling kind of nervous and awkward as I walked into the party, and feeling a little better when I saw his girl, Autumn. Then we all sat and played spades, and then we played hearts, and I started talking to this beautiful girl named Tiffany. As Maceo and I were leaving I asked her if she'd like to grab a coffee sometime, and she smiled at me—a beautiful, luscious smile—and said cool.

I don't even know if Tiffany exists (if she does, I've never met her), and yet I remember speaking with her almost as clearly as I remember studying for my econ test, reading and rereading those formulas, then making a few flash cards and quizzing myself until I became tired and fell asleep.

I've been experiencing these double memories for about five months now. The first time was a few days after I graduated from high school, when my friend Matt gave me a ride home after we'd spent the evening hanging out at the Waffle House. As I was falling asleep that night, though, I remembered walking home from the Waffle House. I had no doubt that I'd actually gone with Matt—it was hot outside, and late, and I didn't feel like walking so I jumped into his car the moment he offered. But I also remembered declining his offer. I remembered walking across the parking lot and down the sidewalk. I remembered repeatedly wiping the sweat off my brow with my forearm. I remembered stepping on branches and leaves and cursing under my breath. I remembered getting momentarily lost after I tried to take a shortcut through a little stand of woods about a mile from my apartment, feeling the fear tiptoe up the back of my neck because I'd forgotten where I was supposed to exit, and then recognizing the big tree with all the odd markings on its base, and stepping out into the moonlight a few moments later, waves of relief rolling through me.

As I lay in bed that night I was confused by the clarity of these alternate images in my mind. Where had they come from? And what was I supposed to do with them? After a while I dismissed them; I assumed that my mind was playing tricks on me because I was tired. Or that I was remembering some earlier walk.

But a couple weeks later I had another double memory. And then another about a month after that. And a few days after that.

Now I experience these double memories about once a day. Most of the time they're trivial—I'll remember marking up an essay draft with a red pen when I know I used a blue pen, and I'll quickly glance at my essay on my desk and sigh with relief when I see those blue marks cascading down the page. Or I'll remember enjoying a cold shower just after I turn the shower off, even though I can't stand cold showers. I always end up turning the shower back on for just a second, to feel if that first burst of water is hot or cold.

I can still tell the difference between the event that actually occurred and its false reverberation in my mind, but it's getting harder.

One of the first things I decided to do once I arrived at Morehouse was to start writing about my life. I wrote a bunch in high school, mostly sci-fi and fantasy stories, but the moment I stepped on campus I had this intense urge to write about the major events that led me here. And I didn't really think much about it because all these words came flowing out of me, I don't know from where, full sentences and paragraphs and pages, and I felt compelled to write everything down. But I think I can admit to myself now that I'm transcribing these memories because they are from a time when I did not have to question if I had experienced something or not. I never understood before what a gift that was.

I think about my mom all the time and what happened to her. I have no idea when she began to feel sick, if at some point she experienced what I'm experiencing now. If these double memories are just the first steps in a long, painful process that will only end when I have completely lost myself to confusion, depression, and paranoia.

I can't stop thinking that maybe my mother passed down whatever was wrong with her to me.

I feel this fear most acutely when I look in the mirror. The funny thing is that I avoided looking at mirrors for years because I was so ashamed of the way I looked. Growing up as a dark-skinned kid in a series of all-white towns will do that to you. And then one day when I was ten, my grandmother told me that I was a young man, and that I had to learn how to focus on myself. I took her words seriously, and literally, and I spent a great deal of time looking in mirrors after that, even though for many years I saw nothing more than an awkward, timid boy staring back. Yet today, when I look in a mirror— say the mirror that's positioned right above the desk on which I'm writing this—I can see that, finally, my grandmother is right. I am a young man. But I can't really say that I feel any connection with the person who's staring back at me. He appears calm and proud and assured, which is crazy because inside I feel constantly sad and overwhelmed. Sometimes I can't help but think that this person in the mirror is the one who's living this alternate life that I can't stop remembering.

Since I began writing about my life a few months ago, I've also spent a lot of time thinking about my father and the way he raised Tayo and me. All those books he made us read, the shows he made us watch, his obsession with our grades. It's obvious to me now that his entire objective was to mold each of us into his idea of the perfect black man. No—his objective was to mold each of us into men whose blackness would not prevent us from succeeding. Tayo stopped taking him seriously by the time we became teenagers, but as I grew older I internalized his desires for me. I began to take note of the people he admired and those he dismissed. In time, following his lead, I created a template for the kind of black man I wanted to be.

I studied the way that Sidney Poitier held his head when he spoke. Tall, erect, proud. I studied Hakeem Olajuwon's walk, loping and graceful. I studied Bryant Gumbel—he always seemed so poised during interviews, and sometimes after I finished watching him on TV I'd run to the bathroom and practice asking questions as if I were him.

I've only just realized that I was studying a particular kind of black man. The kind of black men whom my father and I admired were inevitably those whom had been mostly or completely accepted by mainstream American society. Simply put, they had been accepted by white people. I didn't know it at the time, but by modeling myself after these men I was choosing to become a very specific kind of person. The kind of black man who was nonthreatening and well-behaved. The kind of black man who was successful and benign. These are acceptable traits, of course, but I rarely explored anything beyond these boundaries. My objective during those years was to be embraced by others, to somehow make myself conventional in spite of everything about me that was foreign. There were times when I considered following another path, away from my father and convention, there were times when I did so for a day, a week, sometimes months at a time. There were times when I dared to dream of the life that I'd have if the choice were entirely mine, but I always found my way back to reality. I think of those times often now, and I wonder where I would be if I'd had the fortitude to keep moving.

I guess I've finally realized that the person I see in the mirror is the person I'm supposed to be, and not the person I actually am.

Maybe this is why my mind is rebelling against me. Maybe my mind is trying to push beyond the restrictions I've placed on myself for so long—restrictions that were meant to ensure that everyone I met would be at ease in my presence, at the expense of whatever may have been actually happening inside.

I need to find a way to connect myself to something secure inside me, something that's genuine and true. Maybe things will get better for me if I figure out how to do this.

I need to tell this person in the mirror a story. Not the kind of story that's well-behaved and logical—in other words, not the kind of story that resembles me. I need to tell him the kind of story I would tell myself if no one was listening.

I think I'll tell him about my stepmother. I haven't really been able to write about her or Femi or Ade because I know how their story ends. Everything I've written about my stepmother so far makes her seem like a sidekick or a sitcom wife. I have no idea how I'm supposed to write about her with compassion—to write her as a fully human character—when I know in the end she will leave my father and Tayo and me, that we will never hear from her or her sons again.

Maybe if I just write to this person in the mirror about her, this person who is and isn't me, maybe if I just tell him how I feel, maybe it won't be so difficult. Maybe I'll be able to do it.

You Recognized the Love That Would Never Be

Before anything else, you studied her eyes. They were large, brown, and oval. You saw something like love flickering from them. She had just arrived from Nigeria after almost a day of flying, and later you refused to admit this to yourself because it felt like something of a betrayal, and because of everything that would happen afterward, but for some reason, at that moment, as you studied her eyes, you decided that she had come to America just for you, to claim you as her own.

You decided she was the mother you had always wanted. Something told you she was a dream come true.

Even as you smiled, though, you noticed that the warmth in her eyes had already begun to fade. You ignored this. You told yourself she needed a chance to get to know you. That you needed to show her you were worthy of her love.

You set about trying to impress her every way you could. You did all your chores, you worked hard in school, and you made sure the love in your eyes was visible to her at all times. But her eyes remained blank and cold even as she cared for you like you had always been hers. You persisted. And you kept your attention on her eyes, always her eyes, hoping the love inside would show itself to you.

Sometimes you tried to convince yourself the love in her eyes was merely shy. You tried your best to draw it out—you washed more dishes and folded more clothes. You earned more As, and read more books. Nothing changed. After a few months you only saw her love when she interacted with her two sons, who had come from Nigeria with her. In the quick moments it took for her to move her head from one position to another, from one child, hers, to another, not hers, the love in her eyes would leap out and disappear, and you always wondered *where did it go?*

One cold Saturday in January, about five months after your new family arrived from Nigeria, your father announced he was taking your new brothers out for a drive. You and Tayo were left with your new mother in your cold, cold house, the heater having lost its nerve a few days before. She summoned you to the washroom in the evening, after a long day of silence, around the time you were wondering if your father and new brothers would ever come back. She pointed to a stack of laundry by the dryer.

"Tunde, who folded that?"

You looked at the clothes. They looked as if they had been folded nicely but her tone suggested that something was wrong. You decided to answer honestly.

"I did, ma."

"What did I tell you about mixing the towels with the shirts, Tunde?"

You looked at the towel stack and noticed that there

were, indeed, a few shirts mixed in. It seemed a trivial matter to you, but when you looked at her, your face cradling a tentative smile, her eyes stared back at you, through you, utterly humorless, flint-like in their intensity and willingness to spark fire.

"I'm sorry, ma, I'll—"

And before the sentence could complete its course, she slapped you. Hard. Your heartbeat rose quickly to your left cheek and began to beat there, loudly, as you tried to figure out what had happened. You held your face in your hand, and your skin felt so raw that it was as if you were holding something else, something slightly heavy and warm, like a newborn. You looked, again, into her eyes, and when you saw nothing but your own hatred staring back at you, you excused yourself and went to your room and cried. Tayo came by and asked you what had happened, but you couldn't tell him through the sobs.

After you finished crying you touched your face once more. Through the door you could hear a scrap of music. You did not recognize the tune, but for some reason it made you smile. And this smile—the suddenness of its appearance, how instantly it lifted your soul—prompted you to remember what your grandmother had told you the last time you spoke with her on the phone. That you were a young man now.

That you had to focus on yourself.

You thought about all the things you had done to make your new mother happy, all the chores and good grades and everything else. How none of this had worked.

As you sat there smiling, you decided she was selfish. You decided she was cruel. You decided you had no choice but to turn away from her.

You decided to follow your grandmother's advice. To focus on yourself. To discover the things that made your heart beat faster and slower. The things that gave you joy.

Do you remember how, in the days and weeks after your new mother arrived from Nigeria, she was always on the phone? Do you remember how at first she called Nigeria just once a week, and then every couple days, and then every day? She always called right around dinnertime. After she had set the table and called you and the rest of your family to the kitchen she would sit and close her eyes. Your father would pray for a few minutes, and then he would rub his stomach and begin to eat, always complimenting her cooking as he smacked loudly. Mom would smile as you and your siblings ate. Her food remained untouched. Then she would excuse herself, always asking your father for permission first, always promising she would return shortly. And then nothing but silence as your mother closed the door of their bedroom. You often heard your parents arguing about how expensive it was to call Nigeria, but your father never said a word when she left. He stared down at his food. His smile grew sour and withered away. Soon you would hear your mother shout or laugh or sigh, and her hurried speech, her voice somehow lighter and higher than it ever was when she spoke with you, when she spoke with anyone in your house. When she was on the phone you always had the feeling that you were hearing her real voice, that the version of herself she presented to you and the rest of your family was somehow inauthentic, that she was actually talkative and loud and funny and happy, but that this other person was just out of reach, that she would never show herself to you, that this person, her real self, would always remain behind a closed door.

A few days after your mother slapped you, your father told you and your siblings that you could no longer listen to American pop music. He said there was nothing of value in the music on the radio, that if you listened you would abandon his teachings. So you and Tayo and Femi listened to popular Nigerian music instead and, occasionally, American gospel.

You already loved Nigerian music, juju especially, with its dense polyrhythms—rhythms so intricate and layered that you quickly grew tired of merely listening to the drums converse with one another. You always wanted to hold the music, to feel it pulse and thrum against your palms, to feel it wriggle defiantly away. You grew to love gospel as well, never knowing that you were listening to a very particular brand of gospel, not the soulful, eloquent phrasings of the civil rights heroes you would later read about in class—Mahalia Jackson and Paul Robeson never sang in your house—but the leaner, lighter, more accessible gospel that accompanied 1980s-style televangelism. Your father had a particular fondness for an old cassette tape of gospel standards by Tammy Faye Bakker. You listened to the tape multiple times a day, your father's careworn voice accompanying her every note, you and your brothers listening in silence.

Of course, you had a dim awareness of what was playing on the radio. Your father could not shield your ears at all times, and when you went shopping, or to school, and later when you were out with your father selling ice cream, you would hear fragments of the forbidden music. You greedily collected each fragment you heard, hoarding the bits and pieces in your head as if they were shining shards of gold, and every night before you went to sleep you would carefully piece the notes together, working as hard as you could to force the discordant melodies into a kind of unison. You were trying to distill a lullaby from the bits of rap and rock and soul, something that would soothe you, ease you to sleep.

Once, while you and Femi were cleaning the ancient entertainment system in your living room, you came upon a stash of records tucked behind boxes of tapes and books. Your mother was at work, as always, and your father was out with Tayo and Ade. You pulled the records out and peered at the covers. You saw many records by artists you had heard of—Whitney Houston, Lionel Ritchie, and Whodini, for example—and many more by artists you knew nothing about. You spent the most time examining a record by the Ohio Players. On the cover a man was lying atop a bald, strikingly attractive woman. The woman was holding a knife to the man's back. Her mouth was curled in ecstasy. You and Femi stared at each other for a moment. You felt warm and excited, but you couldn't find the language to wrap around the feeling. Femi pulled the record from your hand and held it close to his face. Then he began to chuckle.

"So then why did your father say that we can't listen to American music," he asked. "Why can he if we can't?"

You did not know what to say. You were shocked because he had said "your father." Like he wanted nothing to do with him. Femi stared at you like he was waiting for an answer. When you said nothing he dropped the record and walked away. You picked it up and put it back where you'd found it.

You discovered other clues that your father loved music as much as you did, that no matter what he said he could not help himself; he had to listen to everything. Sometimes, when you were in the car with your father, and he was feeling down, he would slip a tape into the cassette player. You weren't really familiar with the songs, but the singers had American accents and they weren't singing about God. You saw your father mouthing every lyric, though you'd look quickly away whenever he glanced in your direction.

You grew to love singing more than anything else. You joined three choirs at your elementary school, and you were a soloist in each one. Each song you sang seemed to lift you, note by note, from the fog of pop-culture ignorance your father had allowed to settle on your life.

———

Do you remember that day when you saw your father holding your mother close in the living room, wiping tears away from her cheeks? You had just come home from choir practice, and Femi was the only other person there. You had never seen her cry before. You didn't know what to do. And do you remember how Femi rushed to her side and tried to hug her, but your father screamed at him to go to his room?

Do you remember the way Femi looked at your father? You saw a dense, dark hatred swirling in his eyes. They stared at each other until your father took your mother to their room and closed the door. Femi clenched his fists and shook his head slowly. For a moment you were afraid something bad was about to happen. But nothing did. And do you remember when, just two days later, you saw your mother sitting on the couch, holding a thin blue letter close to her chest? Her eyes were closed. Ade was curled up next to her, sucking his thumb. Your father appeared suddenly and told you and your brothers to leave her alone. You and Tayo began to move away, but Femi ignored him and remained behind. You sat on your bed and read an old edition of *Sports Illustrated* with Hakeem Olajuwon on the cover. Your hands would not stop shaking. Then Femi raged in and said that Mom's cousin had died. That she was sad because she didn't have enough money to go back to Nigeria for her funeral.

Femi looked like he was about to cry himself. He said that America was full of shit. That nothing was turning out the way he'd hoped.

You knew he was actually talking about your father.

In the following weeks your mother cried and continued to cry. Do you remember how miserable she looked? The house grew silent. You watched the leaves outside your bedroom window turn yellow, then brown.

One bright September afternoon, about two years after Mom and your new brothers arrived from Nigeria, your father announced that you were moving to Texas. Dad told you that he and Mom would find better jobs in Texas and you would have a chance to learn more about your Nigerian heritage since there were many more Nigerians in Texas than Utah. Mom nodded as he spoke. She did not say a word. Then your father cleared his throat. He said the move to Texas would also be good for Ade, who would be starting school soon. "I've heard that Texas schools are very good," he said. "Ade is a smart child. He needs the very best." Your mother smiled wide. You father grinned and folded his arms. The last time you'd seen him so happy was when he'd sold a hundred dollars' worth of ice cream during a single stop. Ade began clapping his hands. "I'm going to school soon! I'm going to school soon," he sang. He was jumping up and down. He was four now, and he no longer looked like your father. Nor did he look like your mother. He looked like someone else, someone you had never met before. Someone you would never meet.

You were sad about moving to Texas, but excited too, because you had seen Texas in the movies, and you imagined open spaces, and scores of cattle, and Southern accents, and something different from the cloistered life you were leading. So you packed for days and said your goodbyes, and then you were on the road, riding in the back of your father's ice cream truck with the rest of your siblings, the Wasatch Mountains slowly diminishing behind you.

Your family arrived in Cirrilo, Texas, after almost a day of driving. You moved in with a friend of your father's from college. Dad's friend stashed you and your brothers in the small guest bedroom, and you spent all evening fighting for scraps of floor space. On your first night in Texas, after you said your prayers and before your father went to sleep, he passed you a cheap clock radio. He told you you'd have to use it to get up for school since he would be leaving quite early every morning to find work.

That night, after setting the alarm, you roamed the stations until you came across a hip-hop and R&B station. The sounds you heard then, flowing in waves from the speaker as if through a broken dam, almost drowned you. You cupped the radio to your ear, and when your brothers heard the whispering sounds they gathered around, even little Ade, snot dripping from his nose, a raggedy teddy bear in his hand. You listened with them, eyes closed.

You heard Boyz II Men sing for the first time that night. The DJ said "And now 'Thank You' by the Boyz!" and then . . .

The song startled you, excited you, overwhelmed you. You couldn't recognize the various elements of it, the doo-wop, new jack swing, the soul. And yet it was, without a doubt, the most beautiful thing you had ever heard.

During your first few days in Texas, you fell for Boyz II Men, Mariah Carey, Aaron Hall, Whitney Houston, and Michael Jackson. Every night, after you and your brothers prayed, you would flick on the clock radio, close your eyes, and listen. You studied the tunes that emerged from that cheap clock radio harder than anything you were supposed to be studying in school. Soon you had many melodies to accompany your dreams. You no longer needed to create your own personal lullabies.

Sometimes, when you were listening, time seemed to stop and accelerate simultaneously, sometimes the music embraced you and caused you to forget where you were, who you were, sometimes you felt the music had created you so you could acknowledge its existence. The first time you felt this way was when you heard Lauryn Hill sing. Something came loose in you after you heard "Killing Me Softly," and you remember wishing you could hear that song, and only that song, again and again.

Do you remember how hard Tayo worked to gain your stepmother's love? In the beginning she treated you and Tayo the same. When she looked at him her eyes remained blank and cold. When he prepared her favorite okra soup she nodded and smiled vacantly. She slapped him once for bouncing a basketball inside the house. On the rare occasions when she hugged him her eyes seemed to be elsewhere, to be searching for Femi or Ade, anyone but him.

Do you remember how pleased you were that she was

rejecting him just as she had rejected you? Each time she did so you felt a little less alone. You knew it was wrong to enjoy someone else's misfortune. This did not stop you.

But Tayo refused to give up. Do you remember how he continued to hug her, regardless of what her eyes said? Do you remember how he continued to smile up at her after he finished his chores? Do you remember how he tickled her feet, and how she laughed, at first as if she was annoyed, and then genuinely? Although it took some time, you saw that the coldness in her eyes was beginning to fade away. That she was beginning to warm to him.

Soon Tayo began to tell you things about her life that you had never known. Do you remember that day when you and Tayo were playing basketball at the park after school and he casually mentioned that your stepmother's husband had died in a car accident shortly after Ade was born? You stopped dribbling because you were so shocked. You were breathing hard. As you reached into your pocket for your inhaler Tayo swiped the ball from you and raced to the other side. He stopped at the free-throw line and arced a beautiful shot through the net. He raised his arms. "I won again!" he yelled.

Do you remember how angry you were with him at that moment? You couldn't tell if you were upset because you were finally beginning to realize he was better at basketball than you, or because he knew things about her you had never guessed.

Do you remember the other fragments of information Tayo shared with you in the following days? That her favorite show was *Dateline*, that she, too, had played basketball when she was young, that she had met your father at a house party in Lagos many years before they decided to get married, that she knew your mother, your real mother, when they were both young girls though they had never been friends, that she missed Nigeria more than she ever thought she would, that every night she dreamed of going back?

Do you remember how each revelation caused you to become angrier with Tayo? How—though you could never explain this feeling—you felt that he had betrayed you? That he was somehow betraying your other mother, your real mother?

Do you remember?

Your family moved to another apartment a few months later. By now you and your brothers were listening to the radio constantly. Your mother and father, surprisingly, had little to say. You made sure not to listen around them, but on the rare occasions when your father caught you he would yell at you. You would bow your head while he shouted for a few minutes, but he never took the clock radio when he was done, so you assumed he just didn't want you to play your music when he was around. You were more than happy to oblige. Your mother sometimes stood by your bedroom door when the radio was on, but she never said a word. She would merely observe you for a few minutes, and then she'd walk away.

You and Mom no longer spoke to each other as mother and son. You addressed her like she was a random elder to whom you were to show deference and respect, and she responded as if you were a child in need of food, shelter, and occasional correction. On the few occasions when you were in the car with her you didn't speak much, but she allowed you to fiddle with the car radio as much as you desired.

In the car she smiled at you every now and then. You felt incredible when she did so. You were surprised to learn that she knew so many of the songs on the radio. Sometimes both of you hummed together.

Sometimes when you were in the car with your mother you wondered what kind of music your other mother, your real mother, listened to. Thinking about her felt like an illegal act. Your father had told you and Tayo to move on, to leave her in the past. But sometimes you couldn't help yourself. You wondered if she liked American music. Or juju. Or something else. You wondered if she would hum with you. You wondered if she would let you sing for her. Maybe at the end she would clap loudly and kiss each of your cheeks.

Do you remember that time your father slapped Femi? Dad had just come home from work. You could tell from the way he was walking that he'd had a tough day. He was working at a temp agency because nothing else was available, and sometimes he came home with a smile on his face after spending a day in an office, and other times he came home with dark sweat patches under his arms, smelling like oil and grime.

Today he smelled horrible, like sweat and oil and sour lemons.

Femi was watching TV, which was technically OK because he had finished his homework, but you and your siblings knew to stay out of your father's way after work, to give him a few minutes to cool down. Femi did not move.

"What are you doing there?"

"All my work is done," Femi said. He said this to the TV.

I know you will never forget the way your father's eyes went red, how he strode across the living room and raised his hand. The sound is perfectly preserved in your memory, a loud, stunning pop of noise, like a wet kiss, and Femi's shocked look afterward, his hand cradling his face. And before the tears come you look up and see your mother walking into the room, the expression that crosses her face. You cannot identify it because you have never seen it before. But you know something has changed. Inside her. You're not sure what it is. But you know.

You made a few friends during your first couple months of school in Cirrilo, and you discovered there were others who loved Boyz II Men and the Fugees as much as you did. One friend, Scott, even handed you Boyz II Men's latest CD after class one day, only a couple days after you'd mentioned to him how much you loved their music. You thanked him so many times that his face suddenly bloomed a bright shade of red.

Unfortunately, you had no CD player, so the disc sat on your dresser, collecting dust. You pulled out the liner

notes every night after dinner, and you spent your evenings memorizing each lyric, each song, each producer,
and you tried to compose the rest of the album—the songs
that weren't on the radio—in your head. You even tried
to sing the lyrics the way you thought the Boyz would
sing them. Sometimes during these moments you dared to
imagine that you were a singer with your own songs on
the radio, inspiring others as Boyz II Men and Lauryn had
inspired you, because this is what you actually wanted to
do with your life, but you knew this would never happen.
You had been raised to be practical. To be conventional
and conventionally successful. This is why you did not
ask your father for a CD player—you knew this would
be a step too far. You knew he would tell you to focus
on your studies, to stop dreaming stupid dreams, that he
might even decide to forbid you from listening to music
altogether. So instead you cherished your one CD and polished it nightly. You packed up your dreams and hid them
from yourself.

Somehow, she knew. On your twelfth birthday, after
your family had sung for you and before your father opened
up your birthday pizza, your mother tapped his arm and
told him to wait. She disappeared into their bedroom and
emerged a few moments later with a big box wrapped in
brown paper. You and your brothers stared at it.

"What's the meaning of this?" Dad said, and Mom
pointed at you.

"It's for you. Open it." she said, and she motioned toward
the box.

"Mom, how many times have I told you that we cannot do this, that if we buy something for one child we must buy something for everyone . . ." Dad said, but he trailed off when Mom touched his arm again, and then everyone looked at you.

You stood before the box, and after looking up at your parents again for permission—your father did not return your glance, and Mom nodded encouragingly—you carefully opened the package. Inside was a mini-stereo system with a CD player.

When you looked up at your mother with amazement, hoping for an explanation, she said, simply:

"I knew you wanted it, so I got it for you."

Everything in you melted. You felt lost in love.

But then, for some reason, your heart cooled. You put the box down. "Mom, I can't tell you how much I appreciate this," you said, looking up at her. You saw that she was trying to tell you something with her eyes. "I really needed this."

Your father smiled brightly. Mom nodded.

"I understand," she said. "This is just the beginning."

That night you played your Boyz II Men CD for the first time. You were surprised that many of the melodies you'd never heard matched up almost perfectly with the versions you'd crafted in your head. You looked up to see your stepmother standing in the doorway. She smiled at you. You finally understood what she was saying to you. With her eyes. In that moment you left your room. You left your house, your city, Texas, you left America, you journeyed into the future, you saw how your relationship with her would evolve, what you would become to her.

You saw that she had already decided to leave.

You saw that your time with her was drawing to a close.

You smiled at each other and in her eyes you recognized the love that would never be.

GRANDMA + TUNDE

"Hello, Grandma?"

"Who is this?"

"It's Tunde."

"Ah! Tunde! How are you?"

"I'm fine, ma."

"I must wish you a happy, happy birthday! I'm sorry I didn't call you before. The electricity here isn't reliable."

"Thank you, ma."

"So how are you doing? How is school?"

"School is fine, ma."

"Is your father there?"

"He is at work, ma."

"And where is Tayo?"

"Tayo is at school."

"What is that noise?"

"Oh, I'm sorry. That's my new CD player."

"What did you say? And why aren't you at school?"

"I am sick, ma."

"Ah-ah! What is wrong with you?"

"I just have a cold; I am actually feeling better."

"OK. I will be praying for you. You must get better soon."

"I will, ma."

"All will be well with you."

"Amen."

"Amen."

"Grandma, can I ask you a question?"

"Of course."

"You might get mad at me."

"How can I get mad at you? You are my grandson. There is nothing you could do to me to make me angry."

"Are you sure?"

"Ah-ah! Did I not just say I wouldn't get mad? Ask me your question!"

"OK. I know this might sound weird, but I just read this book about some aliens."

"What are aleens?"

"People from outer space."

"From where?"

"Space."

"Where is space?"

"I mean from the sky. From outside the Earth."

"Which kind books are you reading, now? Is that what they are assigning for you at school?"

"No, I just like to read about them for fun."

"OK-o. I hope you are still keeping up with your studies as you read about the aleens."

"I am, ma."

"So what is your question?"

"Well, I just read this book, and one of the people in the book didn't actually exist—"

"What do you mean?"

"I mean, this guy was talking to another guy on the phone, and he thought the second guy existed, but he found out by the end of the book the second guy wasn't real."

"Does your daddy know you are reading these kind of books? You should be reading your Bible and your schoolbooks. That is all."

"Yes, ma."

"OK. Continue telling me about this man."

"Well, like I said, the first guy discovered that the second guy wasn't alive, that the second guy was just a machine."

"So what is your question?"

"Well . . . when I finished reading the book, it kind of made me think about you."

"Me, ke?"

"Yes. You."

"What do you mean?"

"I mean, I know that you are alive, and that you are real, but I've never seen you."

"And so?"

"So there was a part of me that was wondering if you actually exist. I mean, I know you exist, but I can't prove it."

"What do you need to prove?"

"I mean, I've never even seen a picture of you!"

"You want to see a picture of me?"

"No . . . I mean, yes, I do, but that's not what I'm talking about."

"Tunde, you will have to forgive me, but I don't know what you are saying."

"All I'm saying is how can I know you are real when I never see you? And how can I be sure that Mom still exists when I never even hear from her?"

"Tunde, are we talking right now?"

"Yes, ma."

"And do you feel anything for me?"

"What do you mean?"

"I mean, what do you feel if I tell you that I love you?"

"Well . . . I feel good."

"So what do you think about that feeling?"

"I like it."

"Does it feel real to you?"

"Yes."

"And do you love me?"

"Yes."

"How can you love me if you have never seen me?"

"I don't know. I just do."

"That is right. Sometimes you just have to know. Even if you can't see something with your eyes."

"OK."

"So you understand?"

"I guess."

"Are you sure?"'

"Well . . ."

"So what is still bothering you?"

"Well, I've been having troubles with my memory recently. I know this might not make sense, but I've been remembering things that didn't happen to me. At first these memories were about things I had just experienced, but now

I'm having false memories about earlier periods of my life. I have no idea where they're coming from, but they're vivid. Really vivid. Almost like they are not actually memories, but things that are happening to me right now."

"Like what?"

"Well, like I know for a fact that my stepmother gave me a CD player for my twelfth birthday. I still have the card she gave me. I even called Dad to ask him the other day and he confirmed it. But . . ."

"What is it?"

"Well, for some reason a part of me is convinced that Dad gave it to me right after my stepmom left. I know this isn't right, that it can't possibly be right, but it feels real."

"I see."

"I guess this isn't such a big deal, but this has been happening to me a lot recently and it's really starting to mess with me. This is why I'm writing so much now. I'm trying to record my most important memories as quickly as I can so they remain pure. Like I know that you and I had a conversation about aliens and my biological mother, and I know it was incredibly important to me, but I want to make sure I'm getting it right. I want to make sure I'm remembering you, the real you, and not some version of you that never existed."

"How long has this been happening?"

"A few months, I guess."

"Well, I think the only thing that matters is that I supported you when you were young. And that my words are still supporting you today. That's what memories are for. They are meant to sustain you and refresh you. Always re-

member that your memories are for today, not yesterday.
They change because you change."

"Yes, ma."

"Are you sure you understand?"

"I think so, ma."

"Good. So don't worry yourself. Everything will be fine.

"OK, ma."

"And now I have a question for you."

"Yes?"

"Why are you fighting this?"

"I don't understand."

"You said that you can see things that did not happen to
you as if they did. Tell me why this is bad?"

"Because they aren't my memories."

"Have you considered that this might be a gift?"

"I'm sorry?"

"Has it occurred to you that these other memories are
showing you something important about your life? Something important that you need to know?"

"I hadn't considered that."

"Before you discard them or assume you are sick, why
don't you allow them to speak to you?"

"Because they aren't real, Grandma."

"I am beginning to notice you are very fond of that word.
Maybe that is the American in you. Maybe you should give
them a chance. What is the harm in accepting something that
comes so easily to you?"

"OK, ma. I will try."

"Good."

My father had never been happier. He was working at a mechanic shop and trying to get his ice cream business started up in Cirrilo, and he wasn't really making that much money, but he often told me everything was lining up just the way it should. Just you wait and see, he'd say to me, and then he'd nod rapidly, like nine or ten times in a row, which was something he'd never done before. I knew he was happy because Mom seemed genuinely happy, which I didn't even think was possible. But there she was—laughing at everything, buying cheap-ass toys for each of us, preparing ornate meals each night, doing this weird Nigerian dance all over the house, all flailing arms and jiggly thighs, even picking up my brothers and me from school every now and then. Dad had no clue that she would be leaving him in about three months, but then again how could he? Now that I think about it, I know she was already in love with someone else—that's why her smile was so fluorescent.

Femi and Ade were finally figuring out America, and Femi had lost his accent. They had both memorized all the lyrics to *The Fresh Prince of Bel-Air* theme song by then (even though Dad had forbidden us from watching it—when we asked him why, he told us the black people on that show were not good role models), and whenever they wanted to piss me off they'd corner me and start screaming at the top of their lungs, *NOW THIS IS A STORY/ALL ABOUT HOW/ MY LIFE GOT FLIPPED TURNED UPSIDE DOWN. . . .* I'll admit it: I often fantasized about strangling them. Slowly and methodically. I don't even care how that sounds.

Tayo was happy too—he was the starting point guard on the seventh grade team (I was coming off the bench for the eighth-grade team), and he had figured out all kinds of things that would escape me for at least another decade or so.

Like: how to talk to girls without stuttering like a dumbass.

Like: how to throw a perfect spiral.

Like: how to be black.

This was my main problem. I had no idea how to be black. I mean, I was black, I am black, I can't change that, but I had no idea how to be a black *American*. An African American. Even though I'd spent my entire life in America, I had no idea how to be black like Will Smith, like Michael Jordan, like many of the black people I frequently saw on TV. I always felt somewhat bewildered when I saw them, especially when I saw a group of black people together—at a concert, on a team, at a church service, in a classroom. The way they greeted each other, the way they laughed . . . they seemed to share something in common that was completely lacking in me. The few times I told my father how I felt he responded the same way: he told me not to worry, that if I worked hard enough and became successful, people would want to be like me. I took solace in his words for many years.

Then I started eighth grade. This was in '95. The year I grew almost six inches. The year when Tayo began to transform from what he had been—my clone, basically, Tom Brokaw with an Afro—to this unrecognizable person who walked with a hitch in his step, who used words I didn't understand, who wrote rap lyrics he recited with gusto, who said "What's up?" all the time while jutting his head up just slightly. It looked so damn cool, the head thing. I tried to do it a couple times, in private, but in the mirror I looked like an amateur head banger. Not so cool.

I wasn't the only one who noticed Tayo had changed. My father yelled at him about the way he walked; he asked Tayo if something was wrong with his legs, why he was limping everywhere. Femi started asking him for advice about clothes and girls, and if Tayo wasn't around he'd ask me, but I could tell he wasn't really interested in my answers. And the girls at school began to linger around Tayo between classes and during lunch. One day I even saw him walking down the hallway with an eighth-grader, Rebecca, who I had a crush on. They waved at me as they walked by, and I couldn't help but notice Tayo's broad smile, and how beautiful Rebecca was, how her chest bounced slightly as she moved away from me.

The thing that was most perplexing about Tayo's transformation was that my brothers and I were basically the only black kids in town. Cirrilo, Texas, was just like Hartville, the town in Utah we'd left two years before—they were both small towns with a single police station, a single movie theater, and like zero—OK, maybe one or two—black people. Yet by the middle of the school year I could picture Tayo hanging out with Will and Jazzy Jeff on an episode of *Fresh Prince*; I could even imagine him leaping and swaying on *Soul Train* (a show that I'd only seen once in my life, many years before—it was yet another show that my father had forbidden us from watching).

So what had he done? How had he changed?

I didn't know. But I felt like he'd somehow managed to crack a code to a new, mysterious, thrilling way of living. I wanted to crack that code as well.

I wasn't interested in learning anything from Tayo; he was my younger brother, after all, and how much did he actually know about black people? And besides, I was supposed to be teaching *him* things.

No, I wanted to meet and befriend a black American. Someone my age. Someone who would teach me how to dress and walk. What to say and how to say it. Someone who would be patient with me and teach me how to be in the world.

A black best friend.

But how in the world was I—a kid who was living in nowhere, Texas, a kid who had met only one or two black kids in his entire life—supposed to meet someone like that?

━━━

His name is AJ. AJ Reynolds. I have no idea where he's from. One day he just strolls into my fourth period health class like he's always been there. He's wearing a pair of baggy jeans and a black shirt that has the words **FIGHT THE POWER** emblazoned in red on the front. His hair looks magnificent; the sides of his head are shaved, and rising from the crown of his head is a beautiful column of glistening black. This column is perfectly shaped, not a single curl out of place. As he introduces himself to the class I absently rub my hair, which my mother sheared with our ancient family clippers the night before. I can't help but notice how lopsided my own haircut is, the patches of bald skin beneath the rough, uneven stubble.

At the end of class AJ walks right up to me and stares at my shirt. I look down and see Michael Jackson staring up at me. I'm an MJ fanatic and I've somehow convinced my father to purchase five MJ shirts for me over the past few months, but this MJ is my favorite MJ: his nose is just right—this MJ's gone under the knife only once or twice— and his hair is curly, but not too curly, and his skin is the color of a Werther's Original. MJ is smiling widely, and just below his face a disembodied glove shimmers faintly ("faintly" because even though I've only allowed my mother to wash the shirt two times, most of the glitter has already disappeared).

AJ gazes at me with an odd intensity. I can't tell what he's thinking. Then he smiles.

"Dope shirt," he says.

Is "dope" good or bad? I've heard the word on the radio a few times, but I still can't figure out what it means. Maybe it's something bad—my father once told me that I can never smoke it. But AJ's smile gives me hope. I smile back tentatively. Then AJ sticks out his hand. I do the same, and prepare myself to shake his hand firmly and confidently, just like Dad taught me at the beginning of the school year. Instead, AJ grips and slaps my hand into a series of holds until, somehow, my hand returns to its original position when he's done. He laughs when I stare at my hand as if he's performed a magic trick. He says don't worry, man, I'll teach you. He spends a few moments showing me the mechanics of his special handshake, the exact instant when I'm supposed to clench and release, and the ease, the smoothness, with which I'm supposed to pull everything off.

"Not bad," he says, after I've awkwardly executed his handshake for the fifth time.

"Really?"

"Yeah. You gotta practice, though."

AJ strides out of class and I feel all those eyes behind me, tracking his sauntering steps away from us. I stand there staring at my hand, turning it over like it's a new thing.

That night, after dinner, I call Tayo into our bedroom. He does his head nod thing and then he rubs his eyes. I stick my hand out at him. "Let's go," I say. Tayo glances at my hand, and then back at me.

"What?"

"Come on, man," I say, and once he places his hand in mine I begin to do AJ's handshake. At the end Tayo stares at me, his eyes large with admiration.

"Where did you learn that?"

"Wouldn't you like to know."

"I'm serious," he says. "You have to teach me how to do it."

I spend the next few minutes showing him how to do the handshake. I stumble a couple times but Tayo doesn't notice, or he doesn't care—he listens intently and asks me many questions. I feel special. He hasn't paid this much attention to anything I've said in months.

AJ and I don't speak much in the days following our initial encounter; he doesn't have much time for me because he becomes the most popular kid at Cirrilo Middle School the moment he arrives. A loose knot of humanity buzzes around him wherever he goes, amplifying his every utterance, muffling every other sound but its own sweet drone. He acknowledges me briefly whenever I greet him, nodding and even smiling on occasion, and every now and then we practice his handshake. Sometimes after first period, sometimes in the cafeteria during lunch. Usually, though, AJ turns away after he sees me, his eyes darting around to find the two girls who've already proclaimed their affection for him: Natalie, the prettiest girl in school, and Rebecca, the chestiest.

I'm disappointed that he's too busy to spend any time with me, but I follow him around anyway. I study him from afar. I shadow him during classes, between classes, during gym, everywhere. I watch the way he swaggers slowly from one place to the next, as if he has all the time in the world. I see the way my friends smile at him, their eyes bright and animated, and the way my teachers frown slightly whenever he greets them. I feel how the temperature rises whenever he enters a room, the way everyone leans forward just as he's about to speak. I listen closely to each word he says, and in this way I begin to learn bits and pieces of the strange but beautiful language that AJ speaks so fluently. Words like "fresh" and "dope" and "homie" quickly become a part of my personal lexicon. These words feel leaden in my mouth when I say them, heavy and unnatural, so I repeat them to myself while staring at the mirror. Sometimes I even jab the air for emphasis on certain syllables, just like AJ does.

—

Of all the things I remember from this time in my life, Mom's expanding happiness seems more genuine, more real than anything else. She was generous with her hugs and smiles in a way she had never been. She offered me kind words when I was feeling down. She spoke softly whenever I made a mistake. She and Dad seemed more content than they'd ever been, and even when they bickered it never seemed serious, and usually Mom was teasing Dad (though it always took him a few moments to get the joke).

But I sensed that her happiness had nothing to do with me—even at her happiest she seemed unable to hold my gaze for more than a few seconds. I also had a feeling that her happiness had little to do with my siblings; she didn't really spend much time with any of us, Femi and Ade included, and even when she was around it always seemed like she was on her way somewhere else.

Sometimes during the weekends she would dress up in her Nigerian clothes and ask Dad for the keys to the car. Each outfit was more spectacular than the last, and she'd tell us that she was going to visit a friend in Dallas. I didn't pay much attention to what she was saying though maybe I should have. Every now and then I would stand at the window as she drove away. I wanted to travel to Dallas with her. To learn more about the person she was when she was away from us.

But most of all I wanted to go to Dallas. It was only an hour away, but I had been there only twice, and each time I'd remained for only an hour or so. I wanted to spend more time there. I felt like Dallas was a place where wondrous, impossible things happened. And I knew there were black people there, lots and lots of black people. I wanted to hang out with them.

Even if I somehow made it to Dallas, though, I had no idea how I'd go about meeting black people. And I had no idea what they would think of me.

I meet AJ's parents shortly after he arrives and, unlike their son, they immediately take to me. His father, a gruff, bespectacled man who dresses like an aging college professor—all tweed and ugly ties and wrinkled dress shirts—often volunteers to drive me home after school. AJ's mother hugs me warmly when we see each other for the first time in the school parking lot. Then she holds my face. "You are an incredibly beautiful person," she says.

I feel warm inside for days afterward.

About a month after AJ's arrival, Mrs. Reynolds calls my house out of the blue and asks my father if she can take me to the annual Texas State NAACP Conference in Dallas. Dad's in a good mood, so he consents without asking her a single question. I don't know much about the NAACP, and my father's description ("Oh, it's just a bunch of black people who get together to complain about stuff") isn't really helpful. But I don't care; I'm just excited that I'll be spending an entire day away from my house, hanging with AJ and his mom.

Mrs. Reynolds comes by to pick me up the following morning. She's a tall, thin woman whose hair seems to reside in a different dimension from the rest of her body. Every time I see her something dramatic is happening atop her head—a frizzy 'fro one day, luxuriously straight hair cascading down her slight shoulders the next—but when I open the door on the morning of the conference her hair is in a short, neat, plaited pattern. It's a cold, drizzly day, and she's wearing a long gray coat that reaches almost to the floor. She nods solemnly at me, and when my father wanders by with sleep in his eyes to see me off, she pushes the door open and smiles before mumbling some words in a melodious, incoherent language. My father looks quizzically at me, then back at her. "Excuse me, madame," he says, and she nods and repeats her indecipherable words.

My father glances at me a second time and I shake my head because I have no clue what she's saying. I look around her at AJ in the car, but he's staring at something on his lap, his high-top fade gleaming like an exquisitely polished exclamation point. When I look again a moment later, I see that he's busy playing a Game Boy.

Now Mrs. Reynolds seems confused. She repeats her words a third time, and my father stares at her without comprehension. Mrs. Reynolds stares back at him, and for the first time in the few weeks I've known her I see something like doubt worming its way onto her face.

"Excuse me, sir, but I thought y'all were from Africa?"

"We are," my father says, proudly.

"Well, why didn't you respond?"

"I didn't know what you were saying."

"But I was talking African."

My father bristles, and I look down because I know what's coming next.

"There is no such language as *African*," he says, disgust dripping from his voice, and right then I try to step forward and walk to the car. I want to stop the conversation before it takes control of them and everyone wakes up dazed and wounded, wondering where all the bombs came from, but my father places one of his thick hands on my shoulder. He bolts me to the ground. Mrs. Reynolds plows forward.

"I know there isn't a language called *African*, but I was speaking Swahili. Doesn't everyone in Africa speak Swahili?"

My father steps forward, crouching almost like a lion.

"What did you just say to me, woman? Who told you that?"

"I read it."

"And where did you read it?"

"A few books."

"Well, all of your books are false!" my father thunders, and I recognize the angry power in his voice. I start tapping his hand to remind him where he is, but he shakes me off.

"They aren't false," Mrs. Reynolds replies. "I know what I'm talking about."

My father squeezes my shoulder, and I don't say anything because I'm willing to take the punishment if his anger subsides even a bit. But then Mrs. Reynolds smiles loudly, flashing the kind gap between her two front teeth.

"Ekaaro," she says, and she bows slightly.

I turn around and look up at my father. He frowns and furrows his brow. Mrs. Reynolds is chuckling. "What did you say?" he asks, cautiously.

"Ekaaro," she says again. "Isn't that what your people say to greet each other?" My father shakes his head, and then he begins to smile, and then he blinks rapidly. He utters a quick stream of excited Yoruba. Mrs. Reynolds laughs, and she responds in English.

"I know some Yoruba, but I don't speak very well," she says. "I spent a few months in Nigeria about a decade ago, and I picked up some words while I was there. I try to keep my language skills up by listening to Nigerian music, but it's hard."

My father's face is a portrait of joy. He laughs loudly.

"Ah, you got me!" he says.

"I know, I know," she says. "I just can't help myself with Nigerian men. It's so easy to wind you guys up!"

I hear my dad laughing. "What can I say? My wife says

the same thing. I am guilty as charged." He pauses. "Anyway, don't mind me. Thank you for taking my son to this conference. I really appreciate it. And please feel free to come by whenever you wish. My wife makes wonderful Nigerian food, and there is always an extra place at our table."

"I will, thank you for the offer. And thank you for allowing your son to come with me."

They stare at each other for a few moments, and I start walking again to break their reverie. My father releases my shoulder; he's waving emphatically when I glance back to say bye.

"Stay out as long as you need, and thanks again!" he bellows.

Mrs. Reynolds opens the back door of her car for me and I wait for AJ to move but he shakes his head. "Naw, man, you can have shotgun," he says.

After I've settled I look in the rearview mirror and see AJ bent over his Game Boy. "Why'd it take so long," he says.

"Oh, we were just getting to know each other." Mrs. Reynolds says. She looks at me and winks, and then she reaches over and grabs my hand.

At the conference I see hundreds of black people greeting each other as if they've known each other all their lives. I have no idea where they're from—I've never seen so many black people in one place before. Everyone hugs a few seconds longer than normal, hands remain attached after the shaking is done, and they all stare at each other with a fierce hunger in their eyes. I feel out of place amid the talking and laughing and hunger, especially since Mrs. Reynolds seems to be the center of attention. She drifts around the room, holding people close and pausing every few seconds to pose for a picture with a cluster of excited kids.

After a few moments a loud voice from somewhere above tells us to move to the auditorium. AJ and I find a couple seats close to the stage. I sit and open the glossy program that someone shoved into my hand as I was walking down the aisle. A few seconds later I stare at AJ with my mouth wide open: his mother's name is right there on the first page. Apparently she's the Opening Speaker. I can't believe it. I'm about to ask AJ for an explanation but he's palming his Game Boy again. I look back down at my program.

I turn the page. Printed across the top are the words *"Lift Ev'ry Voice and Sing": Black National Anthem.*

I've never heard of such a thing.

I begin to study the notes of the song to determine if the words fit the melody of the national anthem I grew up with. I hear someone coughing into the microphone and I look up; Mrs. Reynolds is up there in a bright purple and green caftan, and everyone claps even as she raises her hand. She laughs and waves her hand again and again until everyone responds with a respectful silence.

She begins by talking about the history of black people. She tells us that the first humans in the history of the world were from Africa, and how literature and math and science were developed in Africa while white people were living in caves in Europe. She tells us that the first great civilizations in the world were in Africa and that even Jesus Christ was a black man. And then she lists all the things black people invented that white people have taken credit for: Stoplights. Lightbulbs. Gas masks. Potato chips. The telegraph. The cheers grow louder with each invention she names, until she screams "the artificial heart" and everyone rises to their feet.

"We have to reclaim our history!" she cries. "If we don't we won't have a future!"

I've heard many of these things before, but in an entirely different context; my father has often told me that African Americans are fond of creating stories about all the great things they've done because they don't know how to deal with the reality of their lives. I always believed my father, always chuckled under my breath on the rare occasions when one of my teachers brought up the topic of African American inventions in class, but now I can't help it: I jump up and begin clapping as well. I feel a wild sense of triumph coursing through me.

Mrs. Reynolds tells us about the NAACP after we return to our seats. She speaks about the founding of the National Association for the Advancement of Colored People in 1909, and someone named W. E. B. DuBois, and other people I don't know, issues I cannot fully comprehend. But I don't really care about all those names and places and events—

to me, her narrative is most important. The fact that one triumph has always followed another, and that this conference is, in a way, a continuation of the story she is reciting so proudly. Even in Texas, in the middle of Dallas, we are somehow a part of all of that.

I am.

When she finishes she raises a program above her head, and everyone begins to cheer again.

"Before we go any further, we must honor our ancestors, the spirits of all those who have come before, and the spirits of those who shall follow," she says. "We must sing together."

At this point an elderly black woman ascends the steps to the stage and shuffles to the piano at the far end. She begins to play, and after a few bars the entire auditorium joins in.

Lift ev'ry voice and sing, till earth and heaven ring, ring with the harmonies of liberty . . .

I just listen because it feels like the right thing to do. The song sounds nothing like "The Star Spangled Banner." It sounds older, somehow, and more poignant. In their singing I hear pride and affection and joy. I also hear pain and sadness, and a yearning to overcome, especially when they sing the chorus:

Sing a song full of the faith that the dark past has taught us

Sing a song full of the hope that the present has brought us . . .

To my right, I see a tall man peering at his program. His hair is short and wavy. He sings the song with a passion that startles me. Before each verse he sucks in a gallon of air, and in those breaths I see his desire to connect to everyone, to make the moment last. He looks down at me and nods. He's smiling. Tears are glistening on his cheeks. Out of nowhere I close my eyes—almost like I'm praying, but I'm not, or at least I'm not trying to—I close my eyes and I imagine that I have always been here, that I'll always be here, that I'll never leave.

—

One day, when I arrived home from school, I saw my father sitting on the couch in his Saturday clothes. He cleared his throat and asked me to call my brothers and Mom for a family meeting. Once I had done so my father stood and announced that we were moving to Dallas at the end of the summer. He began laughing as he told us that he'd found a new job there, something at a factory that would pay him much more than he earned at the mechanic shop. He also claimed that he would be able to sell ice cream there, that once we settled in he would make even more money than he'd made in Utah. Mom was ecstatic; she leaped up from the couch and gave my father a big hug. Tayo nudged me and when I glanced at him I saw that his eyebrows were raised. I raised mine as well but my heart wasn't in it. We moved all the time, so I should have expected this. But I was furious. What bothered me most was the abruptness of my father's announcement, how resolute he was. I could do nothing to change his mind. I felt like we'd only arrived in Cirrilo. I knew once we left I would never see my friends again, just like I'd never seen any of the other people I'd left behind.

But I was also feeling something I'd never felt before. Was I excited? Not quite. But something close. We were moving to Dallas. Dallas! With each passing second this word grew larger in my mind. Dallas. Dallas. I loved the sound of it. Dallas. We had never lived in a big city before. Only a series of small towns with nothing but dry land and old people and slow-moving cars. In Dallas I would finally be around people who were like me. I knew I was ready for this moment. More than ready.

And I began to frown as my father spoke, because he could never know that I approved of anything he did, but for the first time I could remember I felt like there was a possibility that my life was actually about to begin. My real life, the life I'd always envisioned for myself, the life in which I was popular and good-looking and people gathered around me because they needed to hear every word I had to say. And now I realized that I could only have this life in a place where no one knew me. A place where I could start afresh.

A place like Dallas.

———

AJ and his mother come by for dinner a few days after my father's announcement. My mother prepares an entire spread for them—eba, goat stew, fried plantains, pepper soup, jollof rice, the works—but she claims she's feeling ill a couple hours before they arrive, and she remains in her room the entire night. Tayo's not around either; he's off somewhere playing ball. But the rest of us have a wonderful time. As Mrs. Reynolds and AJ eat I continually scan their faces for flashes of disgust or disappointment, and save for a single exception (AJ eyes the massive hunk of goat meat on his plate with an expression I've never seen before, something akin to surprise, maybe closer to fear, but he quickly recovers, gulping down the meat with a brave smile, the thick, brown liquid trailing down his chin) they seem to enjoy the food. My father puts on some Ebenezer Obey after we finish, and he teaches AJ a few Yoruba phrases. Femi and Ade dance in the living room. Mrs. Reynolds motions to me and I move from my seat to the one next to her. She leans close.

"How do you feel about moving?" she whispers.

I look down at my hands, at the hairs poking through my skin.

"I'm not sure," I say. "I'm kinda sad, but it's weird, because I'm also kinda happy."

She laughs and rubs my back.

"I know you'll miss me," she says. She leans closer. "You have nothing to worry about. You're going to have a great time there." She pauses. "And take care of your father, you hear?" I nod. She reaches down and squeezes my hand. Then she rises and joins my brothers in the living room. She laughs and waves her hands and wiggles her thighs, and then she bops her head to Obey's drums.

At about ten or so, Mrs. Reynolds wipes her brow and sighs. She hugs my brothers and then she announces that she has to get back home before her husband returns from work.

At the door, as Mrs. Reynolds and Dad say goodbye, AJ and I shake hands for the final time. It's a dazzling performance, a duet of holds, snaps, and slaps. I add a tiny flourish at the end, a double-snap–fist-bump combination, and AJ beams at me. It's a moment right out of the movies, the teacher approving the final efforts of the student, the moment just before the scene where the teacher tells the student that he is ready for the trials ahead, whatever they may be. AJ doesn't say this to me—he rushes outside instead, his mother is calling him from the car—but I know that I am ready. Ready for Dallas, for the black kids I'll meet there, for whatever the future will reveal to me, one bright minute at a time.

━━━

I can't keep doing this. If I continue to indulge this impulse, I will definitely lose track of what actually happened to me, and what didn't. And I can't allow that to happen, because then I'd be lost.

I have to remember what's real.

━━━

On my first day at Lyndon B. Johnson High School my first-period teacher asked me to come up to the front so she could introduce me. She stammered as she tried to pronounce my name. It's *Tune-Day*, I said, listlessly. She nodded and continued to speak, and after a few moments I noticed that everyone was staring up at me, that the room had gone silent. I walked slowly to my desk. By the time I sat I could tell that everyone had already forgotten I was there.

The bell rang, and I edged out of my seat. I looked around and saw everyone doing their own thing. I was relieved that no one approached me. I walked slowly toward the door; my bag felt heavy even though it was empty.

My family had arrived in Dallas about a week before, and my father had insisted that my brothers and I take a few days off school in order to unpack and become acquainted with our new lives. We now lived in a cramped three-bedroom apartment in a hulking, decaying edifice on the south side of the city. Our rooms were smaller than we were used to, and our neighbors a good deal closer, but otherwise our new apartment was pretty much like the one we'd just left. The kitchen featured chipped Formica countertops and an oven that didn't work, like our oven in Cirrilo. The bathroom was just as filthy. And the shit-colored carpet in our living room smelled the same—a revolting blend of vomit and mold—even after my father took the rare step of hiring a professional to come by and clean it.

On my first night in Dallas, I slipped outside after the rest of my family had gone to sleep. Partly I did this because I wanted to explore our new neighborhood myself. Once we arrived my father had repeatedly told us that he had moved us into an "emerging neighborhood," which had sounded good, but I hadn't seen anything yet that justified the label.

The other reason I left is because my parents had spent the entire evening arguing with each other. They were so loud that I couldn't really understand what they were saying; their words took flight and flapped angrily over our heads. Up to that point I hadn't spent much time thinking about their relationship, whether they truly loved each other or not. All I knew is that since my stepmother had arrived from Nigeria she and my father had fallen into a natural partnership. At least it seemed so to me. I couldn't really imagine my father with anyone else. Or her. Earlier that week my father had brought home flowers for her, and she'd dropped them in a vase near the window. I caught her staring at them more than once, a smile glimmering to life on her face each time. That first night in Dallas, though, as Mom screamed at my father with all the rage and passion and affection of someone who is begging to be released from something, the love between them, or the lack of love, became the living, pulsing, all-consuming center of my world. Tayo, Femi, Ade, and I just stood there with shock on our faces. I don't think our parents even noticed us. At the end Mom screamed, "He cares about me! And he has money! *Real* money! And he treats me better than you!" And then she strode into their bedroom and slammed the door. Afterward my father looked stricken. Genuinely confused. He followed her into their room after a few minutes, and we didn't hear anything else from them. I went to bed then, we all did, but I couldn't fall asleep. After some time I decided that the only thing that would make me feel better was some fresh air.

Outside the air was a bit cooler than I expected, but there

was enough light for me to see what was going on. Furtively, I began to walk. Up ahead I saw a brigade of low, shining, Popsicle-colored cars inching up the street in front of our building. Where were they going? And what kind of cars were those? They looked bizarre. And menacing. Bright splashes of graffiti glittered from the sides of buildings and on billboards, even the stop sign at the end of our street. I could not read a single word. Maybe I would learn how to read graffiti in school. Across the street was a concrete basketball court where a few kids my age appeared to be playing a sport that resembled basketball, only the sport they were playing was about a million times faster. Was I fast enough to join them?

No, I wasn't. Not now.

With each step I grew more scared, more aware of the fact that I was moving away from where I was supposed to be. Before long I found myself jogging back to my building.

Suddenly I realized that I missed home.

But which home? Home, in my mind, was a jumble of the various places I'd lived. My favorite bookshop in Hartville right next to my favorite pizza place in Cirrilo. Friends from Bountiful and Cirrilo and Hartville laughing and gossiping with one other. The place I missed did not even exist.

When I came back in I saw Mom sitting on the couch. Her round, polished face was lit in flickering fragments by a tiny candle on the table. She was wearing brown sandals and a light-blue wrapper. Her arms looked skinnier than I'd ever seen them.

"Where have you been?"

I didn't have an answer so I just shrugged. She patted the seat next to her. I sat.

She looked miserable. Even her hair seemed to reflect her mood—instead of the Afro that occasionally crowned her head, or the beautiful long hair that poured down her shoulders on most weekends, her hair was in messy plaits. We didn't really say much to each other. She asked me a few questions about the books I was reading and told me what songs on the radio she really liked, but we also sat in silence for stretches of time. She had always been distant, and despite her happiness, or maybe because of it, in the days before we left Cirrilo she had drawn further away from me, from all of us. There were many times when I imagined that I had a different stepmother, that my father had married someone who was consistently kind and more attentive. A motherly *figure* would have been enough, a teacher, the mother of a friend, someone to give me advice, hold my hand every now and then. Yet, despite myself, I still yearned for my stepmother's love. She wasn't the mother I'd always wanted but she was the mother I had, and because I had grown accustomed to her presence I remained hopeful that our relationship would develop, that one day we would even become indispensable to each other.

And now I was sitting next to her. There she was. I can see her chest rising and falling, the faint down on her cheek. There she is.

After about twenty minutes she rose and told me she was going to sleep. Then she reached down and held my face. "I just want you to know that you are a beautiful person," she said. Then she leaned in close. Almost like she was about to kiss me. "Take care of your father, OK?" she said. She looked like she was about to cry. She turned around and walked away. I sat there for a few minutes afterward. Even then I knew. I knew what was about to happen. My heart was beating fast. I wanted to chase after her and hug her. I wanted to run outside and scream as loudly as I could into the night.

A few days later she was gone. Ade and Femi were gone as well. That night my father calmly told Tayo and me that Mom and our brothers were staying with someone else. We asked him what he meant but he just shook his head. Then he told us to finish up our chores like nothing had happened. A rush of shock and panic flooded my chest, a sensation that I recognized from the time my biological mother had become ill and returned to Nigeria seven years before. I couldn't believe that she had left us. I just couldn't. I refused to believe it.

Someone was tapping my shoulder. I turned around and saw a short white kid with blond hair and hazel eyes squinting up at me.

"Hey dude, welcome to Dallas! My name's Sam."

I mumbled my name.

"Yeah, I heard," he said, cheerily. "What does that mean?"

I sighed. I had answered this question countless times in my life. Usually I offered a long response that was part Yoruba etymology and part family history, but on this particular morning I was too tired for all of that. I decided to use my backup response instead:

"It's French."

"Oh."

Sam looked confused, and I enjoyed seeing him try to process what I'd said. He gave up after a few seconds, and we continued into the hallway.

"Well, Mrs. Turner said that you were born in Utah. Cool! My family went skiing there when I was little, to Snowbird. I bet you went there all the time! I bet you guys basically lived there!"

He was smiling widely. I didn't know what to say. We'd never been skiing because my father had always claimed that traveling down a snowy mountain on metal sticks was a stupid, suicidal idea. I'd always suspected that the real reason we'd never been skiing was because my parents were too broke to afford all the equipment. Sam was staring at me, his eyes gleaming with expectation. I knew what he was waiting for.

"Oh, yeah, we went there a couple times," I said. "It was no biggie."

Sam's eyes grew larger. "Wow! You guys were really lucky. So why'd you guys move to Dallas?"

Sam and I continued talking and walking down the hall. I couldn't help but smile.

My next two classes went much better than I expected. Both teachers treated me well, and I was secretly delighted that a few of my classmates seemed genuinely curious about me. Sam was waiting outside my classroom after third period, and I strolled to the cafeteria with him and his friend

John. There were no doors to the cafeteria, just a large space that opened off the main corridor. I stopped walking when we reached the threshold.

The place looked crazy as hell. I saw colors clashing, I heard sounds clashing, I even saw bodies clashing as people casually bumped into one other without saying so much as a word. The kids were burly, and they forked massive portions of steaming food into their big watery mouths.

There were black kids everywhere. More than I had ever seen in one place.

As I stood there, I couldn't shake the feeling that something was pounding me, rhythmically, and although I felt no pain my head was like a broken windshield, each beat inscribing another crack onto my forehead. I looked to the far end of the cafeteria and saw two large speakers hanging from the ceiling on either side, and I realized with a rush of relief and unbelief that the pounding was actually music, that I was meant to be enjoying it in some way.

Sam and John were staring back at me, waving me forward, and I followed them to our apparent destination—a long line that ended a few feet ahead. When I made it to the front I noticed that the lunch ladies—three of them, dressed in white aprons spattered with gobs of tomato paste and hamburger meat—all appeared to be angry for some reason. They dismissively slapped their spoons and spatulas on the trays that were presented to them; they were grunting in a harsh, synchronized beat.

"Hi," I said, trying to sound smooth. "How are you?"

"What do you want?" the lady before me asked, looking haggard and sour, seemingly irritated by my interruption of her slap and scowl rhythm.

"Thanks for asking, and I love your—"

"Look, hurry up! Too many people behind you! Just tell you what ya need!"

"Hamburger."

"There you go."

I sat down to eat, and I was dumping a second handful of surprisingly delicious French fries into my mouth when I felt a hand on my shoulder, near my neck. I glanced at my shoulder and saw a cocoa-colored hand with clean fingernails. I traced the line of cocoa upward—I saw a muscular arm, developed shoulders, a laughing, grimacing face. He had the kind of smile that didn't turn up fully; the far edges of his lips seemed uncertain somehow, forever on the verge of a frown.

"Hey, man, stand up right quick," he said. His voice had dropped, was deep. Mine hadn't, wasn't.

"Why?" I asked, with my newly deepened voice.

"I just wanna see something, man. Stand up for me right quick."

I looked at my new friends for guidance, but they avoided me. They looked everywhere else. I glanced down. That's when I saw him, smiling up at me.

I realized that I'd somehow forgotten about Michael.

I'd caught Tayo staring doubtfully at me as I pulled on my favorite MJ shirt that morning. He shook his head. "I don't think that'll work here," he said. "Don't do it." As he spoke I stared at his beautiful fade. He was wearing his favorite shirt. It was black and it had the words **FIGHT THE POWER** emblazoned in red on the front. I barely recognized him.

He left the room, and I thought about changing my shirt for a sec, but then I decided against it. I knew what I was doing. It was a dope shirt.

"I would like to eat my food if you don't mind," I said.

"Yeah, that's cool, man, I just want you to stand right quick. I wanna see something."

I noticed that a few people were listening to our conversation. I took a deep breath and stood slowly.

"What the fuck are you wearing?" he said.

He was taller than me, and he was wearing a red Bulls basketball jersey with a white 23 stamped on front, a white shirt underneath, and a pair of jeans. His language shocked me, but I knew I had to stand firm.

"What are you talking about?"

"You heard me, man. The fuck you wearing?"

"A shirt."

He leaned his head back and laughed like he was running out of air. A few black kids rose from the surrounding tables to join him.

"You funny, man, you know that? You a funny dude."

"Thanks."

He laughed again, and his friends joined in. I felt like a cinematic attraction. I looked down at MJ. He was still smiling.

"Where'd you get that shirt from, man?"

"My dad bought it for me."

More laughter. Above it I could hear a new song booming from the speakers. Something with a bizarre looping piano riff. It sounded somewhat familiar.

"So your dad dresses you?"

"No, it was a gift."

"And you accepted it?"

His crew howled. All eyes were on me. Cocoa leaned forward suddenly and grabbed my shoulder. "Hey, fool, it's all good; I'm just playing with you."

"I am not a fool," I said, with all the haughtiness I could muster.

Cocoa paused and frowned at me.

"What did you say?"

"I am not a fool."

"Why do you talk like that?"

"Like what?"

"What's your name anyway?"

"It's *Tune-Day*," I said. I was almost whispering.

"What the fuck is a *TUNE-DAY*?" he said. His crew howled again.

"It's my name."

"Where the hell is that from? That sounds like some African shit."

"Yeah, like that Swahili shit that my moms be talkin' during Kwanzaa." This was one of his friends.

Cocoa brightened. "Yeah, all y'all African niggas speak Swahili, right?"

"No."

I wanted to crawl under a rock, under my house, under

my life. I caught Cocoa's eyes and we stared at each other for a few seconds. Then his face softened. At least I thought so.

He shrugged. I smiled. Then I thrust my hand in his direction—a peace offering. He looked at it and then he just stared at me. I put my hand away.

"Something's wrong with you," he said, "but I can't figure out what." He shook his head. Then he pushed me. I fell and my head bounced against the floor. I felt nauseous and dizzy. I blinked. I looked up and saw that everyone around me was cheering and clapping and laughing. There was a tall guy standing next to me. He was nodding with a smile on his face. Someone was playing a piano somewhere, and it felt good in my bones.

I closed my eyes and imagined they were not laughing at me, but with me. I imagined they saw me for who I am, who I wanted to be, and not how I looked or spoke. I imagined that I was not sad and embarrassed, but that I was expanding with happiness, growing larger and larger by the second. I imagined that I had been accepted, that I had become part of something greater than myself.

I imagined that I no longer had to imagine these things.

September 9, 2001
1:12 AM

What do I remember about the rest of high school?

Well, I remember that we moved all the time. At least once a year. Because Dad was so broke and he was always chasing some shitty job. Dad, Tayo, and I moved south from Dallas to Merton, Texas, right after my stepmother and stepbrothers left, and when Dad told us that we'd be moving again at the end of the school year Tayo said that he wasn't going anywhere because he had a girl and he was doing well on the basketball team. He said that he'd already found a family that was willing to care for him in our absence, and that he'd rather die than move again. Surprisingly, incredibly, astoundingly, Dad didn't argue with him. He just said fine and told me to pack my stuff, and I was stunned because Tayo had so easily done something I was unsure I'd ever be able to do: he had defied my father and started down a path of his own making.

I remember that I was far too shy to talk to any girls. I never went on a date, never kissed a girl, maybe I only hugged a girl once or twice.

I remember that I was incredibly lonely. We moved too often for me to make any new friends, and I fell out of touch with all of my friends from Utah. And then Dad stopped paying for long distance, so I stopped talking to Grandma. That was pretty horrible. I missed her so much that I began to make up conversations with her in my head. I spoke to her for hours at a time, and sometimes I convinced myself that we were actually speaking. That we were somehow close to each another despite the fact that she was so far away.

I remember that I spent most of my time missing people. I missed my stepmother and stepbrothers after they left. I missed Tayo after we moved away from Merton. I missed my mom every single moment of every single day.

I remember that we met a few Nigerians here and there, but I never received those lessons about my heritage that my father promised me before we moved to Texas.

I remember my father's anger, how it infected and corroded everything.

I remember that I read constantly, everything, that what I read seemed more important than what was happening in my life.

I remember that I spent countless hours in front of the mirror, trying out different ways of speaking, different personalities. I remember that by the time I became a senior I had somehow learned how to project a version of myself into the world that seemed to delight and impress others (all that time studying Hakeem and Sidney and Bryant helped). I remember admiring and then becoming jealous of this fake version of myself.

I remember writing, always writing, sometimes about my life, but mostly science fiction stories in which my heroes traveled as far away from Earth as they could.

I remember my father's sadness—so dense and intricate and expansive it should have had its own zipcode.

I remember that *The Miseducation of Lauryn Hill* dropped when I was a junior, that I listened to it nonstop until I graduated.

I remember that I applied to a bunch of schools, and that I eventually winnowed my list down to two: Morehouse College and Bates College in Lewiston, Maine. I considered Bates because Mrs. Ross, my favorite librarian, had gone there, she even wrote a letter of recommendation for me, but I felt that Morehouse was where I was supposed to be, and so I ended up here.

I remember lots of things, but I have reached a point where I can no longer trust my memories.

A few days ago I was thinking about high school and it occurred to me that I had never asked Tayo how he felt when we moved away from Merton. We talked on the phone many times in the weeks and months after Dad and I left, and I saw him whenever he was in town for a basketball game, or just to visit, but for some reason that particular topic never came up. So yesterday I decided to call him up and ask him. He laughed and asked if I was kidding. I said no. He asked again, and then he told me that he'd wanted to stay in Merton, but Dad raised so much hell that he decided it wasn't worth the trouble. "Don't you remember?" he said.

I was shocked. And distressed. Why would he claim that he'd moved with us when he didn't? I asked him if he'd lived with Dad and me in the various places we traveled to after Merton, like Carrollton and Irving. He said of course. I asked him specific questions about each place and he answered them easily. I was panicking by this point, so I asked him if he was sure that he'd actually lived with us during those years, or if maybe he was just remembering the times that he'd visited us. He chuckled, but not like he was amused. Like he was uncomfortable. With me, with our conversation, with everything, probably. Then he asked me where I thought he was living now, and suddenly it occurred to me that I had called Dad's apartment to reach him. Now I was at a complete loss. Maybe he was just visiting Dad. Or maybe he moved in after I left, and no one ever told me. I was so confused that I just laughed, I played it off like I'd been kidding all along, and I ended the call as quickly as I could.

I spent the next few hours trying to remember what Tayo had just told me. I tried everything I could to nudge some hidden or long-forgotten memory loose, something that would enable me to recall the past he had described with so much confidence, but all I can remember is being angry with him. Angry that he would willingly separate himself from us. Angry that he had discovered something he cared for more than Dad and me.

And of course I'm questioning everything now. Yesterday I decided to read this entire document for the first time in a long time, and as I read I realized that I'd forgotten much of what I'd written. And though some of it rings true (I never thought I'd be relieved that I remember—in vivid, frightening detail—the moment when my mom became sick) many details seem off-kilter. For example, I remember a different version of my stepmother and stepbrothers' arrival in America. And a different version of their departure from our place in Dallas. And there are other things that I simply can't recall. Like my stepmother giving me a CD player. Or the Hartville City Fair. When I close my eyes and think back to that period I remember that we called city hall countless times that summer, that Dad even enlisted a few of his customers to call on our behalf, but that the city ultimately refused to grant him a vendor's license. What I remember is that Dad was livid for many months afterward, and that we eventually moved to Texas because Dad was convinced that, as he put it, he would never be anything more than a nigger in Utah.

I'm pretty sure this is supposed to be a story about my life, where I've been and what I've done, and I don't know what I'm supposed to do with the fact that so much of it is unrecognizable.

Then there's the fact that my present-day double memories have only become worse. By "worse" I mean that I'm having them more frequently, many times a day now, about all kinds of things. I'm always meeting people I could not have met, visiting places I've never been, and all of it seems real to me, as real as anything I've ever experienced.

What the hell is wrong with me?

Here's the truth, the real truth, something I've always known but have never admitted to myself: with every fiber of my being I feel like I don't belong here. In this room. At this college. In this country. And it's true that my time at Morehouse isn't going the way that I'd hoped, that I'm just as much of an outsider here as I've always been, that all I really do is go to class and then come back to my room and stare at the wall or write, but I mean more than that. When I was younger I used to tell my father and Tayo that I felt like I didn't fit in my skin, and for years I've tried to rationalize this feeling—I've told myself that I'm just not black enough, or American enough, or Nigerian enough. Shortly after I arrived at Morehouse I decided that the problem was that I'd spent my entire life trying to fit into one box or another; I decided I just needed some time to figure myself out. And all these things are probably true, but they aren't quite right. It's hard to explain, but I've always felt like I'm supposed to be somewhere else. I have no idea where that somewhere else is, or how I'd even get there, if it's some other place or time, but I know it's not here.

I've never admitted these things to myself because I always hoped that I'd figure something out, because what's the alternative? The alternative is the way I feel now: lost, bewildered, terrified.

Because how am I supposed to discover who I am if I can't tell the difference between what happened to me and what didn't? If my memories and my actual life experiences are diverging?

Where do I fit?

I need to get some help. I'm not sure from whom, or how, but I need to do find some way to process what is happening to me.

And I need to stop writing. I don't think this is helping anything. I'm getting lost in all of this.

No. I need to write. When I write I have control. If not over my life, then the lives of the people I'm writing about. What I need to do is to stop acting as if I am writing about myself. Since I can't write with any confidence about what happened to me in high school, or even yesterday, I have to abandon the idea that I can write about my life in any meaningful way.

I have to let Tunde go. I have to let him find his own path.

I actually think this is the best thing I can do for myself. Because when I step back and think about this rationally, it makes perfect sense that my memories are going all haywire. I've been focusing my crazy-ass overactive imagination on myself, on my life, so of course I'm remembering all kinds of random things that never happened to me. If I focus on something else, something external like a story about someone who isn't me, I have no doubt that things will return to normal.

In no time at all I will find my way back to the truth of who I am.

The flight ends abruptly—at least it seems so to him. He exits the plane and while everyone else rushes forward to act out their scenes of love and reunification at the arrival gates he heads to a row of chairs near the SuperShuttle kiosk. He sits and pulls his giant earphones over his ears. He's taking a chartered van from Boston to Maine, but the van won't arrive until seven in the morning, thirteen hours away.

He tries again and again to tuck himself into a comfortable position so he can fall asleep, but nothing works. The chair is dreadful—hard and unyielding. He moves to the neighboring chair and it's the same. So he listens to his music as the sun goes down, and he turns up the volume on his CD player when the maintenance men come out of hiding with their brooms and vacuums and large humming machines.

He closes his eyes and imagines himself as the agitated singer who's wailing in his ears. Suddenly he has long hair, piercings everywhere, his white skin merely a canvas for the whims of the various tattoo artists he visits every so often. He wonders if there are any black people who sing rock music. Besides Prince, that is. And Lenny Kravitz. He, himself, sings, but he's fond of hip-hop and R&B though he's only listened to such music for a few years. Now he remembers doing the same thing—listening to as much rap as he could; memorizing lyrics; imagining himself as the artist who paces the stage and defiantly shouts lyrics at hungry crowds—when he moved to Dallas only a few years before. And here he is, on the move again. He wonders, not for the first time, if he's somehow become addicted to the peripatetic lifestyle he experienced as a child. The abrupt moves from one town in Utah to another, then the scramble south to Texas, then the trying on and casting off of various towns until he left home for college. He wonders if he's addicted to the moving or to the studying, or perhaps, even, to the opportunity that distance presents to everyone, a chance to trade in the miles traveled for a new persona, a disguise that becomes who you are the moment you enter a place that has never seen you before.

He blinks—the sun is peering over the horizon. The maintenance men have disappeared into the netherworld from which they emerged. The airport is regaining consciousness. It's a big brain that launches only a single thought into the air again and again, a vision of planes filled with dozens of restless passengers, some of them anxious, others excited at the prospect of flight, separation from earth. He stands, stretches, and walks over to the large windows to watch the airport think. Then he returns to his chair, pulls on his backpack, and walks away from the terminal, dragging his rolling suitcase behind him. He stops at a newspaper kiosk and purchases a package of mints and a couple magazines for the trip to Maine. Then he strolls to the designated pickup area, a rental car stand just outside the large double doors.

He pops a mint and stands bobbing to his music as the air slowly warms. He frequently consults his watch (just a blinking digital face, the plastic straps fell off years ago), pulling it out of his pocket to glance at the numbers before stuffing it back and pulling it out a few moments later. He does this many times before he realizes that someone observing him from afar might find his actions suspicious, or at least a bit strange. He stuffs his strapless watch into his pocket for good and counts the seconds in his head instead.

Five minutes later a young woman approaches from his right. She smiles and squints at the sign above them, then places her suitcase on the ground. She extends her hand.

"My name's Melissa," she says, and they shake on it. She's dressed plainly—she's wearing a brown T-shirt, tight jeans, and flip-flops. Her brown hair is pulled back into a neat ponytail that seems to wiggle as she smiles, even though she isn't moving her head. Her face is clear, pale and fresh. They stare at each other for a few moments, and then he asks her if she's traveling to the same school in Maine. She nods and tells him that she's transferring from the University of Vermont. He tells her that he's an exchange student, and she interrupts him and tries to guess where he's from. Senegal? No, he says. OK, how about Cameroon? He shakes his head and just as he's about tell her that he's from the States, like her, she raises her hand as if they're in class and waves it for a moment. He's confused, but he calls on her all the same. She says "Jamaica" so loud that a few people in the taxi line glance over at them, and when he shakes his head once more she seems disappointed. She asks, finally, where then? He allows a moment for dramatic pause, then he says "Morehouse" with a wide smile on his face. The name hangs in the air between them, then Melissa shakes her head as if she's trying to clear it of something, she says *where?*

They step away from each other and gaze ahead at the long line of cars entering and leaving the airport. They glance at every vehicle as if it might be the one that is supposed to ferry them away. Despite the awkwardness of their first conversation he is eager to pass a test that has yet to be administered, so he slides his earphones over his ears and turns up the volume on his music until he's sure that Melissa can hear it beside him. He does this even though the music is now so loud that it seems as though a band composed solely of energetic cymbal players has taken up residence in his head. Melissa doesn't look in his direction, so he inches closer to her, and when she notices him she smiles and says something but her words are destroyed by the cymbals. He lowers the volume until the lead singer is yelling in a whisper. It is an interesting effect.

"What did you say?"

"I said what are you listening to?"

"Oh nothing, just a little Creed."

"*Creed?*" She says it just like this.

"Yeah, Creed." He cannot tell if her shock is a sign of amazement or disgust.

"Oh." She looks surprised, looks around. Now he is nervous. Isn't Creed a popular band? They have one of the top songs on the charts at the moment, a number he has actually grown to like after much effort on his part.

"Something wrong with Creed?"

"Oh nothing. Well . . . it's nothing. I just met you, y'know?"

"No, it's all good. Just tell me. You don't like them?"

At this Melissa looks around again and leans toward him. She is so close that he can smell her. She smells of soap and evergreens.

"I don't know if Creed is really popular where you're from, but, honestly, they *suck*."

He nods, but to no one in particular.

"Really? Well I kinda like 'em."

"Really?" says Melissa. She smiles again. Her face was made for smiles. "OK, how about this; I'll give you something to listen to, and you pass me that Creed CD and I'll give them another chance?"

He is pleased by the reasonableness of her statement. He opens his CD player and hands the CD over to her, and she pulls a disc from her bag and hands it to him. On the CD the words No Doubt are printed on masking tape in lazy black handwriting. He places the CD in his player and presses play.

The van finally arrives a few minutes later, and they climb in. The driver stops to pick up a couple other students who are bound for the same school, and then the van glides onto the highway, and Logan International Airport recedes behind them. He's trying to enjoy Melissa's CD, but he finds the music quite moody, and he would prefer something a bit more fast-paced. He turns around to see if Melissa has changed her mind about Creed, but she's already fallen asleep. Her mouth is slightly open, her face at peace. He removes Melissa's CD from his player and inserts another CD from his bag, *The Score* by the Fugees. They rap and sing as the van hurtles forward.

He waves at Melissa and the others in the van after the driver drops him off in front of his dorm, Rand Hall. He looks around. Bates College is washed in light. This is the first place he has been where reality actually supersedes expectation, where the static fantasies evoked by color photographs pale in comparison to humming, buzzing, shining life. He doesn't know how to take it all in, so he stands there and allows his senses to collect what they can, but he knows that the information he's receiving from his eyes and nose and ears is a poor facsimile of the life unfolding before him.

Someone taps his shoulder and he whirls around, still dazed, and sees a tall, kind-looking black man standing there.

"Welcome. We've been waiting for you," the man says. "My name is Dr. Bennett and I'm a dean here. I'll be showing you around. But first let me take you up to your room so you can drop your stuff off."

Dr. Bennett picks up one of his bags and they head inside.

They walk up four flights of stairs and all the way to the end of the hallway. Dr. Bennett knocks on the last door on the left. He reaches into his pocket and flips rapidly through a bunch of keys until he finds the right one. The room is quite large—two beds, two desks, and two large windows that look out over campus, on all the sun-drenched happenings below. He dumps his stuff on the bed on the right-hand side of the room and stands there for a moment. Then he turns and they leave.

Together they walk around the campus, and he's delighted to see all those dorms and buildings up close. With each step he feels happier, more assured of his place in the world.

Dr. Bennett accompanies him back to his dorm. There are many people gathered on the lawn on the side of the dorm now, and large metal buckets everywhere, filled with lobsters. He sees people expertly deconstructing the lobsters, the many fingers working quickly over the red shells and pulling soft, yellow-tinted white meat from within. He looks at Dr. Bennett and Dr. Bennett smiles and points ahead to an empty spot on the grass. They sit, and a short woman with steel-gray hair shuffles by and hands a lobster to Dr. Bennett and another one to him. She drops a few napkins on his lap and shuffles away. Without prompting, Dr. Bennett shows him how to break the lobster apart. It's a messy process, and even Dr. Bennett has bits of lobster dripping down his fingers and the sides of his mouth. The effort is worth it, though. The lobster is good. He accepts another lobster from the old woman and tries again, occasionally glancing at Dr. Bennett as he inexpertly cracks it open until he develops a style and rhythm all his own. As they eat, the ancient sun lowers itself, ever so carefully, into a pool of pink light.

He is sitting in someone's room with about ten other students, all of them black. It's close to 9 PM. He wonders why the room is dark, and why—since he arrived at this school four days ago—he's only been around people of color. At first he was fine with this because he felt so comfortable among them. He felt they might teach him things he has always wanted to know. Even now when he glances at them he sees, for only a glimmer of a moment, a view of what he could be. They seem so proud, so confident, but also profoundly unhappy—with their circumstances, themselves, with their school—and he intuitively understands that mutual unhappiness, if it's channeled and dammed, can be used to power the turbine of identity. For even if, in the beginning, one acquires identity by negation—*we are what they are not*—at least it's a start, much better than what he is managing on his own.

And yet. Three days ago he discovered that much of his schedule for the following week had already been planned. Since then he's attended various black solidarity meetings, and black parties, and black book discussions, and now he is tired of it all.

He is also keen to learn about the secret ways of successful white people, and he knows he can achieve this only by infiltrating their social circles, by drinking beers with them, by dating them. And yet here he is, staring at the same black faces, only now something is telling him that he may have misjudged the lot of them.

Here, among these black folk, he detects a kind of determined provincialism. It seems the only thing they wish to discuss is home—the food they ate, the clothes they wore, the music they listened to, the stories they created and traded among themselves. The main currency in these conversations—the only currency, perhaps—is nostalgia. He now senses why it might be so difficult for these people to fit in. It seems they are all more interested in lugging their pasts around with them than stepping into the future. He is uncomfortable. He wonders when he will get another chance to chill with Melissa—he hasn't seen her since he arrived, and he's developed something of a crush on her since.

Now they are talking about music. He has a good idea where this will go—he has grown familiar with the unvarying shapes of their stories. Someone will mention a song that everyone in the room is familiar with, and then that someone will claim to have heard the song long before anyone else. This person will then go on to claim to have been present at the club where the song was first broadcast in public; she might even claim that a relative contributed in some way to the production or promotion of the song. Soon enough, his theory is confirmed: now someone is claiming to have been *in the room* when an especially popular tune—a song that everyone in the room, even him, high on his high horse, loves—was being composed. They are all listening as if an ancient creation tale is being told. He rolls his eyes.

After a few minutes someone suggests they play a game of secrets. The premise is simple: everyone in the room is to tell a secret they've never uttered out loud before. The person with the most salacious secret wins. He does not see the point of this game. He has no desire to divulge any secret in such company—after all, he doesn't know a single person here! How is he expected, then, to give these people access to some dark, closed-off part of himself? In his mind he begins to spin a lie full of abuse, theft, and intrigue, just to see how far he can take it, how long his audience will follow him, when someone across the room begins to speak.

She is confident and carefree, divulging a secret that is so striking and lascivious it must be true. She laughs at various points in her tale and gesticulates in a grand manner, as if addressing an audience of hundreds. He is intrigued. He doesn't know how to feel about her willingness to tell these people such a strange, obscene story. He doesn't know what to think of *her*—her boldness, the fact that she seemingly doesn't care what others in the room might think of her when she's done. She yells and she whispers, she points to various places in the room. She finishes with a vocal flourish, ending her tale on a high note, and everyone laughs and claps afterward. "Don't know how I'm going to top that one," someone says. "Me neither," replies someone else.

He decides to tell a secret of his own—about the time he stole a candy bar from a convenience store. After he's done he hears someone clearing her throat, and then another secret, and then another. Over the course of an hour he hears dozens of secrets—secrets that are actually tales about the kind of people they once were, and how different they are from each other, and how alike. Secrets about who they are now, and who they might become. And what secrets! What stories! So many dark, wonderful, twisted hymns.

At the end they vote, and they decide that the first woman's secret was best. Everyone congratulates her, and he looks over in her direction to nod and maybe smile, but it's too dark. He cannot make out her face. The party breaks up then; it's past midnight and they all have early classes. Someone flips on a light switch and suddenly everything is bright yellow, then individual shapes begin to carve themselves out of light. He looks again to the far side of the room to get a look at her but her back is turned and she's walking out the door.

He is struck by the oddest sensation. He wants to follow her. He looks at the door again and she's already gone. He doesn't even know how she looks, only that she's wearing a purple sweater. He stands and stares ahead until someone taps his shoulder. "Are you all right?" He nods, gathers his things, walks out.

Outside he sees her back. She's walking at a regular pace, and he still feels a desire to track her down. Just then he does something he rarely does. He acts impulsively. He jogs up the path and slows down when he draws close to her. He smiles.

"Quite a story you told in there," he says, summoning all the suave he can.

"You think?" she says, playfully. He can make out her profile now. She seems attractive but he needs to get a better look at her. Maybe he can walk her home. . . .

"Where do you live? I don't mind walking you home. No reason for you to be out here by yourself."

Her laughter is like ice cubes filling up a glass.

"I doubt anything's going to happen to me out here, but I have a better idea. You hungry?"

He's not really hungry.

"Yeah, you?"

"Yeah. There's this burger place just down the street. You wanna go?"

"Sure."

She turns suddenly to the left and soon they are walking over the quad, and then they are off campus, venturing into the dark. He's nervous and somehow she senses his discomfort. "Nothing to worry about," she says, laughing. "If anybody comes for you I'll beat them up."

He has to laugh. She's quick. Then she bumps his thigh with her thigh, and now he's wondering what's happening. She smirks and they continue walking.

After a few minutes they tuck into a small, dingy shop at the edge of town. There are only a couple people inside, one behind the counter and another at a table only a few feet from the door. The man behind the counter greets her warmly by name. She responds in kind, and orders for both of them. He is slightly put off by this, but she laughs. "Trust me, you'll love it," she says. With that she walks toward a table in the back, and they sit. I look at her for the first time.

She has long dreadlocks, a warm smile, and high cheekbones. He can't help but smile at her. They talk about college, high school, elementary school, and then the waiter brings their food, large cheeseburgers with fries, and when he bites into his burger he is surprised by how flavorful it is. He looks up to see the woman smiling at him. "See?" she says. He nods and continues to chew.

They remain mostly silent while they're eating, but they look at each other between bites. When they're done they sit for a moment more, and then the owner of the shop wanders by to tell them he's closing up soon. They thank him for the food and take their leave.

He offers to walk her home and she accepts. On the way they walk close to each other even though it isn't cold outside. He walks her all the way to her door. She turns and they face each other. He doesn't know what to do. She hugs him. He smiles awkwardly and walks away before he can ruin the moment.

When he gets to his room he sees that his roommate, who arrived yesterday, is already asleep. He undresses as quickly and quietly as he can, and just as he is climbing into his bed the phone begins to ring. He jumps and rushes to the phone before it rings a third time.

"Hello?"

"Hello," he whispers.

"Finally!" she exclaims.

He is momentarily confused. Then he realizes that she's on the phone.

"Finally?"

"Yeah, I called every room on the top floor of Rand. I remember you said you lived on the top floor, but I couldn't remember what number you said. You might have a few angry neighbors tomorrow morning."

He laughs, and then he hears his roommate moaning in his sleep, so he pulls the phone cord outside and closes the door. He sits on the floor.

"You called every room?"

"Yeah."

"Why?"

"I just wanted to check up on you, that's all."

"But I just saw you a few minutes ago."

"Well, I miss you."

And he feels something happening inside him.

"I missed you too."

There's a pause. She coughs.

"Well, I also wanted to know what you thought about all that stuff I said before."

"At the restaurant?"

"No. In Jamar's room."

"About your ex?"

"Yeah."

"I don't care."

"Really?"

"Yeah."

And he doesn't.

But he does. He likes her, and when she mentions her secret, now no longer a secret—a secret that, when he thinks about it, isn't really a secret at all, just a story that no one in the room had heard before—that day almost two years ago when she and her boyfriend had sex in the back of a truck at a drive-in theater, other kids looking on and cheering, the few parents there honking their horns and shaking their fists, he feels instantly jealous. He knows this feeling is entirely irrational, and he tries to convince himself that her prior life means nothing to him. But this lie will not stick.

And what about her other secrets? Something tells him that she is transparent, that she embraces life fully. That she is not a guarded person like him, that she will tell him anything he wants to know.

And he wants to know everything. At the same time he does not want to know.

And what about his secrets? If they continue to speak, if she feels even a hint of what he is beginning to feel for her, will she expect him to whisper his insecurities into her ears? The fact that he hates so much about himself, that he wants a smaller nose, skin that's a few shades lighter, that he hates his toes, that he studies so hard because he suspects that the only thing people value about him is his ability to memorize facts and perform well on tests?

That he has never been with a girl.

But she is talking and talking, and he can't help himself, he is talking back. It's the kind of conversation that recognizes itself after a few moments and takes control. They talk and talk for hours, and who knows what they discuss? It's the kind of talking that feels good because your words seem to intertwine with the words of the person you're speaking with. They talk until he notices a few of his dormmates are already up and walking toward the showers. They say goodbye and he hangs up the phone. He lies on his bed for a moment. He smiles to himself. Then he rises to brush his teeth and get dressed.

He goes out to find her.

I love thinking about her. Whenever I'm in class, or walking around the quad, or studying in my room, she's on my mind.

She's everything I ever hoped for.

She's absolutely perfect.

I can't stop thinking that there's no way someone like her could actually be real.

I need her. I don't care about anything else. All I know is that I need to be with her.

She wants to hold my hand in public even though I'd rather not, even though I don't really like doing it, even though there are so many other ways we can show each other love.

I like to show her how much I care about her by messing with her. Hiding her soap. Tapping her nose when she's trying to concentrate. Tickling her when she's trying to fall asleep. That sort of thing.

She's learned my language and so now she plays tricks on me as well. She hides my stuff, teases me as I stomp around my room trying to find my keys, my backpack, my books, her laughter welling up inside me until it comes spilling out of my own mouth. That sort of thing. Why isn't this enough? These private expressions of affection. Why must everyone know what's happening between us? Why must we constantly advertise how we feel about each other? Our love is green and young, its first tendrils tentatively poking up into the air. Maybe too much sun isn't such a good thing now.

She wants to hold my hand in public even though we constantly hold hands when we're in her room, or mine. I don't think I've ever known anyone else's hand so well. Each groove, each nook of it could as well be my own. Our hands fit so perfectly together, like she's a puzzle and I'm the missing piece.

She wants to hold my hand in public even though everyone reacts the same way when they see us. They look at our hands and then they look at us, they peer at us, almost like they're trying to imagine if we'll be holding hands this time next week or next year. "Will they last," their eyes say. Also "Do they fit?" Also: "How did he manage to snag her?" When we're outside holding hands I can feel all those eyes boring into me, questioning me, undermining me, and she just walks along like everything is beautiful in the world, and this makes me so angry that sometimes it's hard for me to breathe.

She wants to hold my hand in public even though we've only been dating for like, what, two months? Shouldn't we at least hit the six-month mark before all the gratuitous PDA? Aren't we jinxing ourselves? What's wrong with walking close to each another, maybe even her slipping her arm around mine every now and then? Why the permanence—the inescapability—of handholding?

She wants to hold my hand in public even though there are all these other fine women out here. I see them all the time when we're out, and it seems like more of them appear when we're holding hands. It's like the moment we start holding hands some alarm somewhere goes off, and all the finest women at this college—in this city, in this state—come out to watch us. They tease me with their eyes, they smile flirtatious, untouchable smiles. They wear tight, transparent clothes, they wink at me and show me what I could have if I would just let go of her.

She wants to hold my hand in public even though she

could be holding anyone else's hand. Really, she could. She's so beautiful and so confident, everyone knows her, everyone thinks better of me because I'm with her. So why does she want to hold my hand? All these other men who eye her so aggressively—does she not see them? Or is she pretending that she doesn't see them? Maybe she does see them, maybe she holds their hands when I'm not around. Maybe all of this is some kind of ruse, maybe there's a camera trailing me, maybe one day I'll turn on the TV and see the last *two* months of my life—the happiest moments I've ever had on this green earth—were just a big-ass prank. Once I see it I'll laugh along with it, I'll have to, because why did I ever believe that any of this was real?

She wants to hold my hand in public even though I don't deserve it. I don't deserve the way I feel right now. I don't deserve this joy, this peace, this sense that we are the product of some long equation that has been winding itself through the years, that we, us, are a destination. That we have arrived where we were meant to be, and other things will find us too. Success. Children. Hope.

She wants to hold my hand in public even though I am ugly. I am unsightly, tarnished. My face is a sad collection of odds and ends that were rejected from the faces that were fashioned before mine. There is nothing pleasing in my appearance, and not much pleasing about me, so why does she insist on grasping my hand so tightly?

She wants to hold my hand in public even though the very act of holding hands is an affirmation of our mutual belief in the impossible. Can we afford to believe so dangerously and so wildly in an uncharted future? Both of us come from poverty. Both of us barely made it here. These dreams that nestle in the space between our hands—can we afford to keep them there? Will they survive? Shouldn't we just cast them away—and each other—before we're damaged by the inevitable calamities that feature so largely in our lives?

She wants to hold my hands in public even though I think I love her. Everything I've loved in my life has been destroyed, has destroyed itself. I think I love her but I don't think we'll survive as a couple—I don't think *she'll* survive—if we continue to hold hands, because handholding must be some kind of signal to the universe that we are falling for each other, and if the universe receives that signal I'm afraid we'll be destroyed sometime soon. We have to keep our love at a level that is just beneath love, whatever that is. That's the only way we'll survive this.

She wants to hold my hand in public even though she's held many hands before mine. She told me she's been dating dudes since she was in middle school. How many hands is that? How did they feel?

Do my hands make her feel safe? And if they don't, what am I supposed to do?

She wants to hold my hand in public even though I've told her so many of my fears, and some of the mistakes I've made. She often holds my hand when we're talking, as if her holding will ease more information out of me, and as I'm talking I'll look down at our entwined hands and wonder if she actually has any clue what she's getting herself into. If she cares.

She wanted to hold my hand in public until I told her a few days ago that I didn't want to hold hands anymore. She looked at me with fear and defiance in her eyes. "Why?" I told her that I didn't feel comfortable doing it all the time. "Why?" I muttered something about my culture, my parents' culture, but she knew that I wasn't telling the entire truth. "Why?" So I told her. "I just want to be sure," I said. I wasn't being clear, but she seemed to understand. She nodded and dropped my hands and left my room.

We did not speak for one, two, three, four days. And then she called and asked what I was doing. I'd never been so relieved. I rushed over and gave her a hug and told her I was ready to hold her hand as long as she wants, wherever she wants. She barely managed a smile. And that's how it's been for the past few days, us walking and talking all over campus, us not holding hands.

My eyes are filled with words.
My tears are waterlogged
Apologies. Please
Forgive me.

One night I wake up and she's there, breathing slowly next to me.

I reach over, slip my hand under hers. One by one her fingers curl over mine.

Her face.

Her face is just as I imagined it.

Especially her lips.

Sensuous. Shapely. Full.

"Tell me a joke."

"I don't really have any jokes."

"Are you serious?"

"I'm not a jokester."

"OK, but you must have one in your back pocket or something."

"Nope. My back pocket is empty."

"OK, that was a joke, I guess. But corny."

"A joke is a joke."

"Come on . . . give it a try."

"Why are we doing this in the dark?"

"So you won't have any inhibitions."

"I'm not afraid to tell jokes."

"But maybe you are."

"Not really."

"OK, then, give it a shot."

"Um. OK. What do you get when you cross a turtle and a porcupine?"

"What?"

"A slowpoke."

"Soooooo bad."

"But you laughed."

"Yeah, I did."

"What would you do if someone gave you a million dollars right now?"

"Like just randomly?"

"Yeah."

"Like if someone just came up to me and handed me a check?"

"If you require that level of specificity, then yes."

"I'm not sure. I've never really thought about that before."

"Really?"

"Yeah, really."

"That's pretty weird."

"OK, then, tell me what you'd do."

"I thought you'd never ask. First, I'd give half of it away immediately."

"I see you're trying to show me up."

"And then I'd take the other half and just fly away with you somewhere. Anywhere, really. It wouldn't have to be a beach or anything like that. Wouldn't it be amazing if we could just escape everything and just be together and not have to worry about money or anything like that? Like wouldn't it be amazing if we could just start our own thing somewhere? I'd give just about anything for that."

She said she loves me

She said it twice

I love you, she said

I want you to know that I love you

Her love is everything I have been waiting for

She loves me

She said it twice

Now the joy of my world is in

Noelle

Noelle. Noelle. Noelle. Noelle. Noelle. Noelle. Noelle.
Noelle. Noelle. Noelle. Noelle. Noelle. Noelle. Noelle.
Noelle. Noelle. Noelle. Noelle. Noelle. Noelle. Noelle.
Noelle. Noelle. Noelle Noelle. Noelle. Noelle. Noelle.
Noelle. Noelle. Noelle. Noelle. Noelle. Noelle. Noelle.
Noelle. Noelle. Noelle. Noelle. Noelle. Noelle. Noelle.
Noelle. Noelle. Noelle. Noelle. Noelle. Noelle Noelle.
Noelle. Noelle. Noelle. Noelle. Noelle. Noelle. Noelle.
Noelle. Noelle. Noelle. Noelle. Noelle. Noelle. Noelle.
Noelle. Noelle. Noelle. Noelle. Noelle. Noelle. Noelle.
Noelle. Noelle. Noelle. Noelle. Noelle. Noelle. Noelle.
Noelle. Noelle. Noelle. Noelle. Noelle. Noelle. Noelle.
Noelle. Noelle. Noelle. Noelle. Noelle. Noelle. Noelle.
Noelle. Noelle. Noelle. Noelle. Noelle. Noelle. Noelle.
Noelle. Noelle. Noelle. Noelle. Noelle. Noelle. Noelle.
Noelle. Noelle. Noelle. Noelle. Noelle. Noelle. Noelle.
Noelle. Noelle. Noelle. Noelle. Noelle. Noelle. Noelle.
Noelle. Noelle. Noelle. Noelle. Noelle. Noelle. Noelle.
Noelle. Noelle. Noelle. Noelle. Noelle. Noelle. Noelle.
Noelle. Noelle. Noelle. Noelle. Noelle. Noelle. Noelle.
Noelle. Noelle. Noelle. Noelle. Noelle. Noelle. Noelle.
Noelle. Noelle. Noelle. Noelle. Noelle. Noelle. Noelle.
Noelle. Noelle. Noelle. Noelle. Noelle. Noelle. Noelle.
Noelle. Noelle. Noelle. Noelle. Noelle. Noelle. Noelle.
Noelle. Noelle. Noelle. Noelle. Noelle. Noelle. Noelle.
Noelle. Noelle. Noelle. Noelle. Noelle. Noelle. Noelle.
Noelle. Noelle. Noelle. Noelle. Noelle. Noelle. Noelle.
Noelle. Noelle. Noelle. Noelle. Noelle. Noelle. Noelle.
Noelle. Noelle. Noelle. Noelle. Noelle. Noelle. Noelle.

I love writing her name.

I write it everywhere.

Noelle+Tunde. Noelle+Tunde. Noelle+Tunde. Noelle+Tunde.
Noelle+Tunde. Noelle+Tunde. Noelle+Tunde. Noelle+Tunde.
Noelle+Tunde. Noelle+Tunde. Noelle+Tunde. Noelle+Tunde.
Noelle+Tunde. Noelle+Tunde. Noelle+Tunde. Noelle+Tunde.
Noelle+Tunde. Noelle+Tunde. Noelle+Tunde. Noelle+Tunde.
Noelle+Tunde. Noelle+Tunde. Noelle+Tunde. Noelle+Tunde.
Noelle+Tunde. Noelle+Tunde. Noelle+Tunde. Noelle+Tunde.
Noelle+Tunde. Noelle+Tunde. Noelle+Tunde. Noelle+Tunde.
Noelle+Tunde. Noelle+Tunde. Noelle+Tunde. Noelle+Tunde.
Noelle+Tunde. Noelle+Tunde. Noelle+Tunde. Noelle+Tunde.
Noelle+Tunde. Noelle+Tunde. Noelle+Tunde. Noelle+Tunde.
Noelle+Tunde. Noelle+Tunde. Noelle+Tunde. Noelle+Tunde.
Noelle+Tunde. Noelle+Tunde. Noelle+Tunde. Noelle+Tunde.
Noelle+Tunde. Noelle+Tunde. Noelle+Tunde. Noelle+Tunde.
Noelle+Tunde. Noelle+Tunde. Noelle+Tunde. Noelle+Tunde.
Noelle+Tunde. Noelle+Tunde. Noelle+Tunde. Noelle+Tunde.
Noelle+Tunde. Noelle+Tunde. Noelle+Tunde. Noelle+Tunde.
Noelle+Tunde. Noelle+Tunde. Noelle+Tunde. Noelle+Tunde.
Noelle+Tunde. Noelle+Tunde. Noelle+Tunde. Noelle+Tunde.
Noelle+Tunde. Noelle+Tunde. Noelle+Tunde. Noelle+Tunde.
Noelle+Tunde. Noelle+Tunde. Noelle+Tunde. Noelle+Tunde.
Noelle+Tunde. Noelle+Tunde. Noelle+Tunde. Noelle+Tunde.
Noelle+Tunde. Noelle+Tunde. Noelle+Tunde. Noelle+Tunde.
Noelle+Tunde. Noelle+Tunde. Noelle+Tunde. Noelle+Tunde.
Noelle+Tunde. Noelle+Tunde. Noelle+Tunde. Noelle+Tunde
Noelle+Tunde. Noelle+Tunde. Noelle+Tunde. Noelle+Tunde.
Noelle+Tunde Noelle+Tunde. Noelle+Tunde Noelle+Tunde.
Noelle+Tunde. Noelle+Tunde. Noelle+Tunde. Noelle+Tunde.
Noelle+Tunde. Noelle+Tunde. Noelle+Tunde. Noelle+Tunde.
Noelle+Tunde. Noelle+Tunde. Noelle+Tunde. Noelle+Tunde.

Our names belong together.

We belong together.

Her love makes everything real.

These days and weeks and months

I never spent much time thinking about where time goes. How it passes.

But I can feel it now.

Every second ticking in me when we're together.

Each empty and meaningless moment when we're apart.

"I just want you to know that I've never been happier in my life. Never."

"I feel the same."

"Really?"

"Yes. The exact same."

It's true, I've never been happier in my life

but what happens next?

Where do we go? What do we do? What's the next step? The next chapter?

What happens after happiness?

I know what happens. We fight. We fail. She cheats or I cheat. She falls out of love with me or I fall out of love with her. That's how these things always go.

I can't just let this happen to me.

To us.

I have to be in control.

It will hurt less if I make the first move.

"Do you have to go back?"

"Yes."

"Why?"

"Well, I started at Morehouse. I want to graduate from Morehouse."

"But you can graduate from Bates."

"That's not what I want to do."

"So what about me?"

"I love you."

"Then why are you going back?"

"I just told you."

"But we're perfect here. Why would you even think about messing that up?"

"I'm not trying to mess anything up."

"What are you chasing? Why are you always running? Why can't you just accept when something beautiful is happening?"

"I'm not chasing anything. I just have a feeling that this is the right decision. Why is that so hard to understand?"

"So we're going to do the long-distance thing."

"I don't think it's as bad as you're making it out to be. We'll talk every day. I'll come up and visit. You'll come down and visit."

"It won't be the same. Just watch."

"I told you it wouldn't be the same."

"I don't get why it can't be. I even put off all the lights. Just the way you like. So it's like we're in the dark together."

"But I can't feel you."

"Not even a little?"

"I feel nothing."

"I still can't believe you did this to us."

"I'm sorry. I don't know what's wrong with me. I'll fix it. I promise you. I promise."

Why am I acting this way?

"So what do you think?"

"I'm not sure."

"I think it'll be good for us."

"Don't you think it's kinda early for us to do something like that?"

"I don't know. All I know is that my internship pays really well, so you won't have to worry about finding anything for a while."

"So you're saying I can go down to DC and mooch off you."

"That's not what I'm saying at all. I'm just saying you don't have to be stressed out about trying to find something."

"I have to think about it."

"What's there to think about?"

"Tunde, we're going to be juniors next year. I just declared my major. I have to have a productive summer so that I actually get a job when I graduate."

"But it's DC! There's so much to do! You'll figure it out. We'll figure it out."

"So even if I come down and I get the most amazing job in the world and make a million dollars do you think living together will work for us?"

"I just want to give it a shot. I want to give us a shot."

I'm on my back and Noelle's facing the wall. Her back and my side are touching. She's breathing slow and deep, like she's asleep.

She turns toward me. A few of her locs brush my arm. They feel soft and bristly.

I move closer to her. She lets me kiss her but she pulls back.

"There's something I want to ask you," she says.

"Well, there's something I want to show you," I say, and I touch her chest. She grips my hand and places it back on the bed. "I'm serious," she says.

I laugh. "OK, what's up?"

"It's maybe kinda personal."

"OK."

"This has been on my mind for a while, but I haven't said anything. But you've got this internship and you've been making all this money this summer . . ."

I pull back from her and stare up at the dark ceiling.

"You need some money?"

"No, dummy. I made just as much as you this summer."

"True."

"No. I was thinking that maybe you should visit your mom."

"Who?"

"Your mother. Your real mother."

For a few moments her words are just words. I can't comprehend them. As each word begins to shimmer to life in my head, though, I feel something dark and furious rising in me.

"What did you say?"

"I'm just wondering why you can't use some of your money to visit Nigeria. I mean, you've never been there, and you always say that you never went because your Dad didn't have any money. Well, now you do. Why can't you go now? Why can't you visit your mom?"

"It's not that easy."

"Why not?"

"Cuz I just can't jump on a plane and show up."

"Why not? That's your family."

"But I don't know them like that. I can't even say that I really know them."

"But they're family, right?"

"It doesn't work like that."

"Why not?"

"It just doesn't. And why are you even bringing this up now?"

I feel Noelle moving.

"Tunde, how long have we been dating?"

"What kind of question is that?"

"I'm serious. How long?"

I feel myself getting angrier though I don't know why.

"Is this like *Jeopardy* or some shit?"

"We've been dating for ten months."

"What's your point?"

"The point is that I don't really know you."

"What the hell is that supposed to mean?"

She pauses.

"I know the same you that everyone else knows. The person who's so driven, who's always trying to win something. Who can't stay in one place. But I don't know who you actually are."

I sit up on the bed.

"So you're basically saying that I'm fake?"

"No. I didn't say that."

"Then what are you talking about?"

"I'm talking about the fact that there's a part of you I can't reach. You won't let me get inside. I've tried so hard and I just don't think I can do it."

"OK, so like I said, you think I'm fake as hell and that I'll be less fake if I see my mother. Right? Is that your logic?"

"No, Tunde. I'm saying that you hurt like hell and you might not even know this anymore because you've spent your entire life coping. And I'm saying that you're probably hurting because you've been missing your mom. And I'm saying that you finally have some money and you're a grown-ass man and you don't have to wait for your daddy or anyone else to give you permission to go see her. Just go."

"Well, it's good to hear that all that crazy Iyanla shit you've been listening to is helping you out, but please don't psychoanalyze me."

Noelle sits up, walks across the room, and flicks on the light. At first I'm blind, but then I see her face. It's puffy and her eyes are red. She's wearing my Morehouse T-shirt and nothing else. Her anger has made her even more beautiful, if that's possible. I feel my anger slipping away but I hold it close to me.

"Tunde, fuck you," she says. She reaches by the foot of the bed and grabs a pair of jeans. She shimmies into them and then sits on the chair by the door and slips on her shoes. When she's done she looks at me.

"I've said my piece. Do with it what you will."

She rises and touches the doorknob.

"Where are you going?"

"You're being an asshole and I don't want to be with you right now."

"All right. Whatever. Peace."

Noelle shakes her head. She's still facing the door. She doesn't move.

"If you weren't so obsessed with yourself you'd understand that I'm actually trying to tell you something else."

"So now I'm obsessed with myself?"

She sighs.

"Look, Tunde. I love you. You know that. But I can't be with a robot. You're a robot now. So until you fix that shit, we might have to slow this down."

"So you're breaking up with me?"

"I'm going now," she says, and then she walks out and closes the door behind her and a few moments later another door closes and she's gone.

I turn off the light and go back to the bed. Something comes to me and I leap off the bed and turn the light back on. Yes, she left her purse. I feel a small twinge of satisfaction and hope. Maybe she'll come back soon.

Something tells me she won't.

I miss her so fucking much.

I feel like I'm in a nightmare I can't wake up from.

But she's right. I know she's right.

Grandma, it's been so long since we talked, and I guess that's mostly my fault but I just want you to know that I'm coming to see you soon. I can't tell you how excited I am. Soon I'll be able to see you with my own eyes. So much has changed in my life since we last spoke, and I have so much to tell you that I'm not even sure where I'll start. But I'll figure it out.

2004

I don't know where to look. Directly in front of me, a short wiry man is chopping an animal carcass to bits. The blood is spurting away from the meat in ecstatic waves; it rains down on his skin and shoes. The man looks up and smiles at me. His front teeth are missing. He holds out a slab of flesh in my direction—I shake my head quickly and continue moving forward.

Around me people are screaming from stalls stocked with colors and smells I have never experienced before. To my left and right rickety buildings trickle by, none of them looking particularly hospitable. Or safe. Bright brown faces gawking at me from windows and doorways. Everyone's looking at me as if they know I don't belong.

I peel my shirt from my chest, but it settles back where it was before, fabric and sweat and skin forming a tighter bond. I instinctively reach for my phone but I realize it's useless here, that my data plan did not travel across the Atlantic with me.

I am in Lagos, Nigeria, and I am looking for my mother.

My cousin places his hand on my shoulder and gently nudges me to the left. I pause to glance at him. He looks so much like my mother that maybe he should have been my mother's son. The sun is throbbing above us. It's beating a strange rhythm into my body, something I've never felt before. He points down the street, above the stalls and bobbing heads. I nod and begin to walk, but then my cousin grabs my arm.

"Are you sure you're ready?" he asks.

I smile confidently. It's actually a frown disguised as a smile; I'm sure anyone can see this.

"Yes. I've been waiting for this a long time."

My cousin smiles kindly, but there's something indecipherable there, in the corners of his lips.

We walk past a tall, crumbling building. The exterior is composed of some kind of yellow stone, now chipped in many places, and the roof is tin. Green vines finger every available crevice, and long lizards scoot across the walls, so fast and green that it seems like they've been exiled from an ancient myth. I glance at my cousin again. He smiles ruefully.

Before us stands an arch. We pass beneath it into a wide courtyard. All around us the windows reflect the light, and clothes are strung from lines that crisscross the open space above our heads. I glance up at the sky—the sun is beaming down on me, like a booming flash before an impossibly large camera takes my picture. I have never felt this uncomfortable in the sun, so aware of how conspicuous it is. Has it always been this bright? Maybe a different sun shines over this courtyard. An angrier sun.

I'm afraid I might go blind staring at the sun like this, so I look down, and only now do I realize that the ground beneath my feet is pure gold. The wind is picking up. The windows are screaming with light. I look back up. Now I see the sky peeking through the gaps between the shirts and pants, and I can't tell if the sky is too low, or the clothes too high, because the water-blue air above my head seems close enough to touch, and the clothes are so distant that they look like multicolored clouds, clouds with buttons and zippers and pockets and sleeves.

My thoughts are too loud, too loud. I close my eyes.

In the darkness, with my thoughts bumping against my eyelids, I begin to breathe more easily. I listen to myself inhale and exhale. I feel my cousin again, his love for me passing through his hand into my shoulder. My heart slows some. I feel the heat from the sun settling on my face. I do not have to look up at the sky to know that the sun has returned to its normal size. When I open my eyes I see the clothes swaying gently from the clotheslines and the decaying concrete beneath my feet. The windows are still shining, but benevolently.

I feel my body returning to itself, and now I understand why I lost my composure: I can no longer hear the din of Lagos, the cars and buses and curses and pidgin. My anxious thoughts expanded themselves to make up for the sudden absence of sound. Even now, looking around, the silence is amplifying everything. This silence feels permanent, not like a placeholder for something to come.

Ahead I see a small clearing, and freshly turned earth. Two gravestones are poking up out of the ground. I hear my cousin saying *That is where your grandfather and grandmother are buried* but I don't immediately understand what he means. I keep walking because I want to see my grandfather's grave. I've heard so much about him over the years, and I know that he's the one who constructed the building in which I now stand.

I don't realize that my grandmother is dead until I see the dates on her headstone. I look for my cousin so I can scream at him for not telling me before, but he's already crying.

I kneel and touch the ground. Tears are streaming down my face. My cousin kneels next to me and rubs my back as I trace my fingers over the delicate indentations on my grandmother's headstone. I glance at my grandfather's headstone, which looks just the same, except it indicates that he died twenty years ago. For a moment I can't believe that these austere stones are all that remain of their lives.

A lizard scampers across the space in front of me, chasing something I can't see. My grandmother is the only person I know here, the only person I really know. For my entire life she was just a voice on the phone, someone I loved but never saw. I'm not sure I'll ever accept the fact that she will never be anything more.

My cousin stands, then he lifts me up. We stare at each other.

"I know that you are probably angry with me," he says. "But our uncle told me not to tell you. He said it was better that you find out about our grandmother here with your family, so that we can support you."

"When did she die?

"About two weeks ago. They buried her here last week."

I shake my head slowly.

"What about my mother? Where is she?"

My cousin touches my side. "All in due time. There's something I'd like you to see," he says. "Follow me."

We walk across the courtyard until we come to a wooden door with a metal doorknob. My cousin knocks and someone opens it. Inside people are calling out my name, pulling me in. I look back at my cousin. "This is our family," he says. "They have been waiting for you."

Their smiles are brighter than any I've ever seen in America. Their hugs feel genuine. And the voices I hear greeting me resemble the voices I've heard on the telephone my entire life. Yet their faces are different from what I imagined—each time someone speaks to me they cancel an alternate version of themselves in my mind. I quickly understand that these deaths are necessary: my relatives don't know it, but they are clearing space in me for themselves.

But this isn't the joyful reunion that I expected. They seem happy to see me, but subdued. There are no tears or dramatic gestures. I see my sadness etched on their faces.

The voice, when I first hear it, sounds like a match striking sandpaper. It ignites a calm that spreads quickly around the room. He tells us to hold hands and bow our heads. He begins to pray in Yoruba. I can't fully understand what he's saying. My cousin nudges me and whispers in my ear: "That is our uncle, the oldest member of our family now that our grandmother has died. He is your mother's oldest brother. His name is Uncle Wale." I nod. Have I spoken with him before? I'm not sure.

My uncle says "Amen" and my chest vibrates, like the skin of a drum. I open my eyes, and again I see all those faces,

faces that are so open and warm. Some of them begin to chatter at me again. Others pass by me with tables and chairs, pots and dishes heaping with food, greeting me as they pass.

The voice that greets me now sounds like Aunty Ona, who I speak to once or twice a year, generally on holidays, but she doesn't look anything like I imagined. Her voice is reedy and thin, and each sentence she utters ends with a kind of wail, as if the sentence wishes to continue but there aren't enough words to power it. But the woman standing before me is stout and strong, with a large head and long, vertical scars on each cheek. She leads me back to the courtyard with a hand that is more powerful than my own. And the voice that is teasing me now sounds like Uncle Kayode's—his face somewhat matches the face I created for him so many years ago, but I missed essential details. The nose, for example; Uncle Kayode's nose is slimmer than I imagined from his voice, and he does not have the receding hairline that his doppelgänger, once secure in my head, hid with hats of various sizes.

I'm having this experience again and again, voices and faces initially seem out of focus, but then the blurriness fades. Reality clicks into place.

As I stand here, in the middle of this courtyard, I realize that I'm only beginning to understand what an extended family is. What it means. Back in America I've spent a lifetime parsing the slight physical distinctions between my father and brother and me. Each minute difference is meaningful, for we all resemble one another. Growing up, my brother's lighter skin and my father's short stature seemed to mark the outer boundaries of our genetic possibilities. I found comfort within these boundaries because they clearly marked the space where my family lived. They distinguished us from everyone else. But now, of the fifty or so who are gathered here, I am seeing all kinds of faces, all kinds of noses, so many shades of black, people I would not recognize as family members if they weren't here, and the boundaries of my family extend outward with every glance. And because they all look so dissimilar, and yet alike, I know that I will look at myself differently when I next see a mirror, that there are countless possibilities within me that I am only now discovering.

The courtyard makes more sense with all the food and chatter and tables. I look at the tombstones again. I wish my grandmother were here, standing next to me. She was supposed to guide me through this, to show me what to do. How to be. Someone begins to cough. We settle again, and Uncle Wale announces that we are here to celebrate my arrival, and the departure of Grandma. Now, as before, his is a disembodied voice—I don't know where he is. He says it is not a coincidence that I arrived just after my grandmother died. He tells us that she said I would be coming soon and that my arrival is proof of her closeness to God. Around me voices are murmuring in unison, and this is a sound I've never heard before—all those voices that I cataloged individually and worked so hard to keep apart are seeping into each other, and though I am afraid that I will never be able to disentangle them, I know their voices sound lovelier this way.

Now I hear music. It sounds vaguely like the juju I grew up with, but I have never heard this song. Someone begins to laugh and my cousin directs me toward the long table just ahead. It stretches across the courtyard, piled high with more food than I've ever seen in one place. But I've eaten this food many times—eba and amala and dodo and pepper soup. I stack some jollof rice and moin moin and dodo on my plate and the people who walk past me glance at my food and then at my face and then my food again.

I walk to a table and sit. Around me are cousins and aunts and uncles. I dip my fork into the mound of moin moin on my plate and take a bite. This Nigerian food doesn't taste like Nigerian food. I take another bite. Suddenly I realize that I am tasting Nigerian food for the first time, now, and I also realize that the Nigerian food I ate back in the States was somehow inauthentic—each bite a fuzzy hologram that dissolved into familiarity the moment the food touched my tongue. Then I tasted the American food I was accustomed to: the pancake mix, the canned beans and spinach, the corned beef that I'd had for breakfast with eggs and toast. Now I'm eating more slowly, more carefully, because I want to taste every molecule of this food. If I can't bring anything else back with me to America, if customs seizes all my packages or my bags don't make it across the Atlantic with me, I can still smuggle my tongue's memories back home.

I smile when someone claps my back. A voice exclaims, *So he is a Nigerian after all!* and I laugh along with them. But now I am wondering: How can I possibly be a Nigerian when every Nigerian experience I have had up to this point was made in America?

Yet here I am, in Nigeria. And I know it doesn't make sense, but I do feel as if I have experienced some of these moments before. I have seen these tables assembled in almost perfect rows around me, each with five or six people, the laughter and the food and the sunlight, each leaf bending softly in the breeze. I have felt this sadness, so painful that the only logical response is to act as if I have always felt it. I think of all those times I sat on my bed conjuring faces and places. All those times I created memories of the person I would have been if I'd grown up in Nigeria. I am living in those memories right now. And I'm learning that memory isn't just a catalog of things past; in times of desperation or loss or exile a memory can be a passageway into the future.

As I'm finishing my food I look up and realize that everyone is looking at me. Something solemn is in the air. Silence resettles in the courtyard. It's almost like this courtyard is a giant musical instrument and we are the strings; someone above has been plucking us with abandon for the past few minutes, but this silence is the clearest note.

A little smile unfurls inside of me. This is the part of my trip I have been preparing for since I got here. I know they all want to ask me about my life in America, about all the wonderful treasures that are stored up there. I am ready for this.

"Why did it take you so long to come home?" someone asks me. "Where have you been?" says someone else. "Have you not missed us?" says a third. Others lean forward and begin to talk. "Did you not know that we missed you? How long will you be staying? When will we see you again?" More of them lean forward. "Have you ever thought about living here? When will we see you again? How is your brother doing?" Some of them shift, but the rest remain where they are, staring at me. "When will he be coming? How is your father? When will he come back?" Someone lowers the volume of the music. "Does your father plan on living in America for the rest of his life? They look at me with concern, and then sadness. "Can you tell him that we are waiting for him? When will we see you again? What are you going to do with your life? How often do you pray? Do you pray for us? Do you know how often we pray for you?" I look around for my cousin, but I realize that he has joined them. "When will we see you again? Are you dating anybody? Is she special? Is she the one? How long have you been with her? When will you bring her to Nigeria?" I hear some kind of bird calling in the distance. "Have you finished your studies? When will you graduate? When will we see you again? Have you considered working in Nigeria? Why didn't you tell us you were coming? How do you like Nigeria so far? Is the food to your liking?" Now I hear someone laughing, and her laughter swells into the silence, and suddenly everyone is laughing. "Can you make Nigerian food? Do you have any Nigerian clothes? Why don't you speak Yoruba well?" Anxiety infects their laughter, extinguishes it. "What did you learn about Nigeria in your school? Do your friends know where you are from? What do you think you will tell them about your time here? Have you drunk that before? What do you think of it? When will we see you again?"

I don't know what to say. I am overwhelmed. My words aren't enough.

My cousin appears before me. "Come now," he says. My family watches me depart; I try to discern my destination in their eyes. We enter the building and pass down a dark hallway until we arrive at a door. "Your uncle is there. He wants to speak with you," he says, and then he walks back down the hallway.

I breathe. I close my eyes. I knock.

Someone tells me to come in.

Inside, the room is swaddled in shadows. I can't make out the figure sitting before me until my eyes adjust. After a few seconds he is all that I can see—the dimensions of the room remain invisible to me.

"Sit, sit," he says, and he points to a chair across from his own.

He smiles at me. I can tell that his face must extend a great deal of effort to perform even this simple feat, but the result is wonderful—his wrinkles disappear and his face issues a clean, minimal, toothless grin.

"Do you know who I am?"

He is wearing a pair of trousers and a shirt. I can't make out the pattern because of the darkness. A tall cane rests against the wall beside his chair. He is bald, and his left eye has been smogged over by a cataract. His right hand trembles slightly. His feet are pale and unadorned—they look brand-new.

"Yes, sah."

"Who am I?"

"My uncle, sah."

He smiles again. "Good. Welcome to Nigeria. Come closer to me."

I look around the room, and now I notice a low table to

the left of his chair. I walk slowly across the room and perch on it. My uncle reaches for my hand. We're holding hands and it feels right.

"I am so glad to see you. I was afraid I would die without meeting you."

"I am glad to see you too."

"My mother told me many things about you. But she always told me that you were a good boy. I can see that now."

"Thank you, sah."

"I know that you loved her. And I know that she loves you. She is here with us, even now."

"I know."

"You know that now that my mother has died there is no one to look after your mother. Your grandma is the one who used to visit her every day."

I did not know this. No one ever told me.

"Yes, sah."

"Your cousin will take you to see her soon. Since you are her oldest child you will have to make some arrangements. When are you visiting your father's family?"

"Tomorrow, sah."

"That is good. You can speak with them about it as well. Greet them for me."

"I will, sah."

He nods and doesn't speak. But somehow holding his hand is more than enough.

A few minutes pass.

"Do you mind if I bless you?"

"No, sah."

"Bend your head."

I do as he asks. His hand feels dry and hard on my scalp. I don't recognize a single word that falls from his lips. But they sound like words of power. When he is done he grasps my hand once more.

"You will be seeing your mother soon. I know you are scared, but you mustn't worry."

"Yes, sah."

I inhale deeply.

"Uncle, I have something to ask you."

"Yes, go ahead."

"I don't know what I'm supposed to do. What I'm supposed to say to her."

"Don't worry about that. Your mother is your mother. You will know what you need to say when the time comes."

"Yes, sah."

I've never thought of it this way before. I'm still not quite ready to see her. But this is something.

I look at my uncle and he nods like he agrees with my thoughts.

He grips my hand like he will never see me again.

My cousin ushers me through the maze that extends from my grandparents' section of Lagos to my mother's. Lagos, now familiar to me, seems accessible and cozy as we travel by motorcycle, then taxi, then motorcycle again. We walk down a dark alley, sidestepping open pits, agile four-legged animals, and limbless beggars who stare up at us reverently. We turn left into a small clearing with a crumbling building jousting its way up to a darkening sky. I pause but my cousin continues walking. I follow him inside.

As we walk down the hallway I can just make out the outlines of other human beings standing on either side of us. The whites of their eyes tracking my slow movement through the dark.

My cousin stops before a door on our left. He knocks and steps back. I don't hear a thing behind the door. Someone opens it. She looks at me and I look at her. I do not know her.

She touches her face. *Who are you?* She asks like she's afraid of me. She's wearing a light-blue wrapper and brown sandals. Her arms look so thin. So, so thin. And her face. I can't recognize it but I have always known it. I shake my head slowly. I don't know how to work my voice. She looks, terrified, at my cousin, her eyes pleading for a response.

"This is your son," my cousin says. "He has come all the way from America to see you."

I see my mother trying to decipher my cousin's words. I watch her as she relearns the definition of "son." I can feel myself relearning the pain I thought I had lost somewhere in the past.

But something else is happening to me. Something else.

Something twisting my mother's face. She looks again at my cousin and then at me. She looks harder at me and then her eyes go wide and pure, recognition stripping years away from her face until the woman before me looks like the person she must have been before me, before she became a woman. And then she collapses to the floor and my cousin rushes over to her, laughing, telling her that this is something to be happy about.

She rises slowly with his help. She stares at me once more. Her hand reaches forward.

My first impulse is to flinch, but I catch myself and allow her to stroke my cheek. She rubs one spot insistently, just below my eye, and I am suddenly afraid that she is preparing the spot for something I do not want, a landing strip for an unsolicited kiss. I know I will have to step back if she attempts such a gesture, but she stops and stares at me instead. There are tears building up in her eyes, glassy snowballs gaining heft and speed. I glance away, at the small, dark room behind her. The moonlight is shining down on us through a crack in the ceiling. "Let's go inside," my cousin says.

We walk in and sit on thin, scratchy mats on the floor. My cousin is speaking Yoruba to my mother, and she is staring at me. I'm trying to act like I don't know what he is saying, but of course I do. My mother nods and continues to stare. I look around her room.

There is no electricity here, just a small candle situated on a box in the middle of the room—a thin wedge of light shivers in the dark. I don't glance beyond its grim boundaries; out there lies shame, my mother's and my own. But here, with the shadows roaming our faces, I feel like there's a possibility I might learn something about her.

My cousin is narrating a tale about how we've been planning this surprise for many weeks, how glad I am to see her. She doesn't say a thing. Whenever I glance at her she holds my eyes for just a moment before looking down. When I look away I feel her heavy gaze on my face.

I wonder if she is OK. I wonder if she understands any

of this. I wonder if, to her, I'm merely an oddity from the past, or a figment of her addled imagination that has somehow gained life. If I am just another hallucination. When I was younger I often woke up to my mother's screams in the middle of the night, and then my father's soft whispers. Sometimes this went on for only a few minutes, but usually these conversations lasted the whole night, and then my father would smile in the morning while handing me a lunch bag for school. Behind him the door to their bedroom would be closed. I often wondered if my mother was still asleep, or if my father had somehow managed to cure her, if only for the day. It occurs to me now, as I sit here, that I have finally entered my parents' bedroom, and I only had to travel across the span of sixteen years and six thousand miles to get here. And that she is the same person I would have seen back then—a silent figure who does not recognize me.

My cousin has been talking. "What do you think?" he says. His face implores me to say yes, so I do, though I don't know what he asked me. He hurries outside and I hear him whispering some Yoruba into his cell phone. My mother remains where she is. Looking at me like she isn't looking at me. I want to get the hell out of here.

My cousin rushes back in. "She's coming!" he yells. Now I wonder if I've joined my mother in her serene hallucination. I ask who and my cousin winces. "My mother! Your auntie!" he says. My aunt. Yet another stranger I'm supposed to greet with familiarity and love.

My aunt bounds in a few minutes later, panting. She is thicker than my mother, her face much rounder. At first I don't think she and my mother look anything alike, but when she reaches down to hug my mother I see the resemblance—same round nose, same full lips, same small chin. Now I see that they could actually be twins; the only real difference between them is that my aunt's face seems more vibrant. Comparing her face to my mother's, I can see what happiness does to a face, how it sharpens it, and how sadness can flatten the softer parts of a face, and how anger, too, remolds a face in its image, leaving an imprint of its presence even as a face expresses something else. Looking at them together, it occurs to me that our faces are meant to provide an ongoing transcription of every emotion we have ever felt. And that's why my mother's face is so vacant—for too long hers has been a vessel of loss.

My aunt walks across the darkness and I rise to hug her.

"I'm sorry I wasn't able to meet you at my father's house," she says. "I had to work late today."

She stares at me and smiles.

"Do you remember me?" she asks, full of confidence.

"No," I say.

"Well, you were a little boy when I traveled to Utah. How could you?"

My aunt looks at my mother. "You cannot imagine how happy your mother is now. This is the day that she has been waiting for her entire life. I can tell you that she has never been happier."

My mother looks the same.

"There were times when I would invite her over to my house, and she would be playing with my children and then she would just go to the corner and cry. Sometimes I would try to comfort her but she would always brush me away. And we have both been devastated since your grandmother died. And now, imagine, she is seeing her first son after so many years! Look how happy she is!"

Now my mother searches for something on her wrapper. She finds it, glances at it, and flips it away.

My aunt continues, undeterred. I look at my cousin. He shrugs. I squat back down to the floor, and something loud and juicy rips free of my body. Suddenly I feel light. Relieved. And then a smell; something reeks of rotten eggs. I can't help but grimace, and I look around to see who the hell would pass gas at a time like this, and my mother and cousin and aunt are looking at me the same way.

We are all silent. The smell blooms.

My mother begins to laugh. The sound is so startling at first that I think she's in pain. But no—her entire body is quaking with glee.

She rises and crosses the room. My cousin moves without a word, and my mother sits next to me. She leans her head on my shoulder, her laughter winding its way out of her. The rest of us are shocked, and we look at each other with expressions of concern and curiosity. My mother keeps laughing at my shoulder. She's moving so vigorously that I catch a whiff of her hair. I'm relieved that it smells normal, that it smells like hair, despite its disheveled appearance, the thinning strands of it pointing in every direction, her hair illustrating—in my mind, anyway—the random trajectories of her harried thoughts.

My mother reaches a hand behind me and begins to rub

my back. I look at my cousin and ask him with my eyes what I should do. He shrugs again. My aunt is staring at my mother with her mouth wide open. My mother, still laughing, rises and pulls me up after her. She walks out the door, into the night, and I follow her.

The air is brisk, and the stars above are shining with the same ferocity that they do everywhere else I've been. As my mother pulls me insistently along, dragging me to a fate I cannot even anticipate, I derive some solace from the idea that there is nothing my mother can do to me—no harm or good deed—that these stars, wrapped in their robes of impenetrable darkness, have not seen before.

We're walking fast, and suddenly I am a six-year-old in Salt Lake City, walking up and down the streets as my mother drags me along from one errand to another, because now, like then, I don't know where she is taking me, and now, like then, I am struggling to keep up with her, though I am a full foot taller. My mother looks back at me and flashes a huge smile. I can't remember if this is a good smile or one I should be afraid of.

We stop abruptly in front of a shack that is leaning away from a large dilapidated building. The lone window is boarded up, and the words THIS HOUSE IS NOT FOR SALE are spray-painted above the window in eccentric purple. My mother hops up to the stoop and pulls me beside her. She begins to knock. No one answers. She knocks faster, louder, and I look around, afraid that someone might come out and see us. If she is having an episode I don't know what I'm supposed to do.

The door finally cracks open. A tired old face stares at me with utter incomprehension. My mother steps in front of me, and the door swings open. "Theresa!" My mother smiles bashfully, then she grabs my hand and pulls me closer. "This is my son. He has just arrived from America."

The woman's face crumples. She looks at me like I'm a supernatural figure. She gestures toward the darkness inside her home. "Come in, come in," she says.

My mother shakes her head. "No. There is something else I want from you." My mother drops my hand and unravels the edge of her wrapper. She produces a few colored bills from the folds inside, and sorts them in her hand. Her hand shakes as she extends a few bills to the woman. "Can I have one Fanta?"

The woman looks at the money as if it is poisoned. "Put that away. For you I always have something." She closes the door and I look down at my mother. Her lips are pursed. They might soon burst apart.

The door opens. The woman passes the Fanta to my mother, and my mother hands it to me. Instantly my hand cools, and then my arm. Condensation trails down the glass on all sides. My mother pulls the Fanta from my hand and opens the top with her teeth, and then she hands it back to me.

"Drink it," she says. "This will help with your stomach."

I do not like soda; I can't remember the last time I actually drank one. But I don't have much of a choice, not now. I tip the soda toward my mouth and swallow deeply. The moment I stop I feel the bubbles coming up my nose and throat, the dreaded feeling. But then I feel my mother rubbing my back, and I hear her encouraging me to drink more.

"Don't stop now," she says. "Drink until you have finished it. Then everything will be OK."

I gulp the Fanta down. My mother watches me eagerly.

When I'm done my mother takes the empty bottle from me and hands it over to the woman. The woman takes it hesitantly. "Are you sure you don't want to come in?" she says. My mother shakes her head and tells her that we have somewhere to go. Then she takes my hand and we proceed into the darkness. I look behind us to glance at the woman once more. I have no idea what my face is telling her, but she shakes her head, and then she recedes into her house. The door closes.

We walk back up the alley, and then onto a street I do not recognize. And then another street, and then another. I have given up trying to keep track of where we are.

The world is surprisingly quiet here. Every single building that we pass is dark, but I can feel so many lives humming inside each one. My mother's pace slows some, but she continues to move. She hasn't looked at me once since we left the Fanta woman's house.

Finally she stops. Across the street from us is an empty thoroughfare. A long gutter runs parallel to the sidewalk on which we are standing. There are car parts strewn all over the place: exhaust pipes on the sidewalk, alternators and radiators spread across the road. License plates dot the walls of the structures around us. Nothing stirs.

Something about this place, this time in my life, feels familiar.

My mother sits on the edge of the sidewalk. She pulls my hand until I'm sitting next to her. Then she leans into me.

"Remember when we used to do this?"

Despite my feelings of familiarity I can't remember anything that resembles this moment. I do remember occasionally sitting with my mother on the couch in our apartment, and later on the floor at the women's shelter. I remember trying my best to distract her so that she would forget to hurt me.

But now I feel safe.

A forgotten memory slips through the cracks. My mother is lying next to me on my bed and whispering a story into my ear. The story is about a talking turtle that wants to learn how to fly. I have heard this story many, many times, but what I love most is the way my mother's hot breath feels against my neck, and the way her words gain life in my mind, the turtle trying and failing and trying again, and then climbing onto the back of a friendly seagull and drifting up through the clouds toward the sun.

I glance down at my mother's head because I want to see if she's up for a conversation. There are so many questions I would like to ask her. There's so much I need to know. Her chest rises and falls. She is asleep.

I look around. I have no idea how to get back to her place. My mother seems content and I don't want to wake her up. I don't want to shake her out of her dreams.

I stand and lift my mother into my arms. She settles into me. I walk carefully, picking my way through the debris on the streets. There is no one here who can help us.

I will get us back home.

Acknowledgments

I started writing this novel when I served as a fellow at the Institute for Policy Studies. Special thanks to Emira Woods, Dedrick Asante-Muhammad, and Marc Raskin, who served as my mentors while I was there, and John Cavanaugh for his consistent help. Also to Ethelbert Miller for starting me down this road, Abdul Ali for the nudge, and Gore Vidal, Saul Landau, Sarah Browning, and Ashawna Hailey for the pep talks.

Shout-out to Helon Habila for reading the first chapter of this novel back in 2012, and for telling me that I should keep doing this writing thing.

To Jessica Powell—thanks for being such a supportive writing partner for so many years.

And to Josephine Reed for putting me on the radio and connecting me to so many writers.

To *Transition Magazine* for publishing my work before anyone else, and the Hurston/Wright Foundation and Marita Golden for providing me with a space to explore my artistry.

Much love to the Callaloo Creative Writing Workshop and the Kimbilio Writers' Workshop—two spaces where I felt safe sharing my work and where I learned a great deal about myself and creating art.

The Caine Prize for African Writing has been especially

generous to me—thank you for the recognition, and for the continued support over the years.

To Georgetown University, and especially the Lannan Center for Poetics and Social Practice, for providing me with the funding and space to complete the first draft.

To the good folks at Politics and Prose—thank you for not kicking me out all those times when I was copying the text of the books I was too broke to buy into my notebooks. I'm so thankful!

To the taxpayers of the United States of America for subsidizing my countless trips to the Hirshhorn Museum and Sculpture Garden, the National Gallery of Art, the National Museum of African American History and Culture, the National Museum of African Art, and the Smithsonian American Art Museum—I would not have finished this book without you.

To the various folks who have supported me and believed in me through the years—Akwe Amosu, Chris Eaglin, **Ralph Eubanks, Wil Haygood,** Sy Henderson, Chris Ingram, Kemi Ingram, Jason Jacobs, Ezra Jones, Robert Mallett, Valerie Mallett, Arshad Mohammed, Juliana Montgomery, Christina Nelson, Lois Quam, there are so many more . . . thank you.

To all my work colleagues who have accepted my many absences over the years—in particular Joanne O'Rourke Hindman and Nina Mojiri-Azad. And a special shout-out to Steve Harris for being such a great boss, and Maurice Jones for giving me a shot.

To Maria Massie—thanks for taking on this book and

for never giving up.

To the editorial, publicity, and production teams at Simon & Schuster—thanks for being so patient with me, and for your fine work.

To Carina Guiterman—thanks so much for helping me to get this over the finish line. And Lashanda Anakwah for your support and enthusiasm.

To Ira Silverberg—you pushed me and pushed me and I'm incredibly grateful that I had a chance to work with you. You're the editor I prayed for.

To Ola, Gbenga, Lanre, and Bisola—thanks for being such great siblings, and for keeping me honest.

To my parents for all their love and support and for sacrificing so much. Dad and Mom and Mom—I can't thank you enough.

To Funmi, for bringing so much joy into my life.

And Stephanie—well, you have my heart.

About the Author

TOPE FOLARIN is a Nigerian American writer based in Washington, DC. He won the Caine Prize for African Writing in 2013 and was shortlisted once again in 2016. He was also recently named to the Africa39 list of the most promising African writers under forty. His work has been featured in various literary journals, including *Callaloo, Transition Magazine,* and the *Virginia Quarterly Review*. He was educated at Morehouse College and the University of Oxford, where he earned two master's degrees as a Rhodes Scholar.

A PARTICULAR
KIND OF
BLACK MAN

BY TOPE FOLARIN

This reading group guide for *A Particular Kind of Black Man*
includes an introduction, discussion questions, and ideas for
enhancing your book club. The suggested questions are in-
tended to help your reading group find new and interesting
angles and topics for your discussion. We hope that these
ideas will enrich your conversation and increase your enjoy-
ment of the book.

Introduction

Living in small-town Utah has always been an uneasy fit for Tunde Akinola's family, especially for his Nigerian-born parents. Though Tunde speaks English with a western accent, he can't escape the children who rub his skin and ask why the black won't come off. As he struggles to fit in and find his place in the world, he finds little solace from his parents, who are grappling with their own issues.

Tunde's father, ever the optimist, works tirelessly chasing his American dream while his wife, lonely in Utah without family and friends, sinks deeper into schizophrenia. Then one otherwise-ordinary morning, Tunde's mother wakes him with a hug, bundles him and his baby brother into the car, and takes them away from the only home they've ever known.

But running away doesn't bring her, or her children, any relief from the demons that plague her; once Tunde's father tracks them down, she flees to Nigeria, and Tunde never feels at home again. He spends the rest of his childhood and young adulthood searching for connection—to the wary stepmother and stepbrothers he gains when his father remarries; to the Utah residents who mock his father's accent; to his Texas middle school's crowd of African Americans; to fellow students at a historically black college. In so doing, he discovers something that sends him on a journey away from everything he has known.

Sweeping, stirring, and perspective-shifting, *A Particular Kind of Black Man* is a beautiful and poignant exploration of the meaning of memory, manhood, home, and identity as seen through the eyes of a first-generation Nigerian American.

Topics & Questions for Discussion

1. Consider the title of Folarin's novel, *A Particular Kind of Black Man*. Is Folarin referring to a specific character, or a more general population? Both? How did you interpret the title within the scheme of the novel?

2. Young Tunde and his family are often the black people in their neighborhood. On Tunde's first day of school as a kindergartner, a classmate is shocked that the "black" won't come off Tunde's skin. It's around this same time that an elderly white woman tells Tunde that he can get into heaven if he serves her on earth. How do these experiences set the tone for the novel? How do they affect Tunde?

3. Tunde's mother suffers from schizophrenia, an illness that makes her question her own sense of reality. How does the idea of "reality" play out in the rest of the novel?

4. After Tunde's mother leaves her family behind for Nigeria, Tunde's father attempts to bring home a "new mother" from Nigeria, twice. Why do you think it's so important for him to have a wife and a mother to his children? Do you think his decision ultimately

benefits Tunde and Tayo, or hurts them? Would you have made the same choice if you were in his shoes?

5. The idea of the American Dream plays a huge role in the novel, particularly for Tunde's father. How does he attempt to achieve the American Dream? Is he successful? Discuss the meaning of the American Dream with your book club members. Do you think that it's an attainable goal? How might the American Dream be different now than it was fifty (or even ten) years ago?

6. On page 99, Folarin fast-forwards through time to Tunde as a college student, experiencing frightening "double memories" (p. 102) that make him fearful he is falling victim to the same disease as his mother. Why do you think Tunde is beginning to experience these double memories? What do they represent?

7. Why do you think Folarin writes parts of his novel like a journal or a memoir? Could Tunde's story be a true story? Why or why not? What elements of the story (if any) "remind" you that this is fiction?

8. Tunde's stepmother gives him a mini-stereo system for his twelfth birthday: a gift that, given her lack of relationship with Tunde and Tunde's father's disapproval of pop music, is surprising. Why do you think

she chooses to give Tunde this peace offering? What does it foreshadow about her future in America?

9. "I had no idea how to be black. I mean, I was black . . . but I had no idea how to be a black *American*. . . . The way they greeted each other, the way they laughed . . . they seemed to share something in common that was completely lacking in me" (p. 134). Discuss the theme of identity in *A Particular Kind of Black Man*, and the struggles that come with being a black American and an African American.

10. Tunde's visit to the Texas State NAACP Conference in Dallas is transformative. Why do you think this is such a powerful moment for him? Why does he find belonging here when he struggles to find it everywhere else?

11. When Tunde transfers from Morehouse to Bates, he falls in love for the first time, but soon he second-guesses himself. "What happens after happiness?" (pp. 214–217). Why does Tunde try to sabotage his relationship with Noelle? Do you think he succeeds?

12. This book is written using a variety of different styles, tenses, and tools. At times it reads like a memoir; at other times, like poetry. Discuss with your book group what the experience of reading the novel was like.

13. *A Particular Black Man* ends with Tunde and his mother's reunion in Nigeria. If Folarin were to add an epilogue to the book, what do you think would have happened?

14. Return to the epigraph at the novel's beginning and consider it within the context of the book as a whole. How does Tunde "create" himself in all of the places he moves throughout the novel? Do you think he has found himself by the book's end, or does he still have work to do? How at peace with himself—and his past— is he by the time he carries his mother home?

Enhance Your Book Club

1. Food plays an important role in the novel throughout the novel. By the time Tunde finally reaches Nigeria, he gets the opportunity to try "real" Nigerian food for the first time: "Eba and amala and dodo and pepper soup . . . jollof rice and moin moin" (p. 244). Visit a local Nigerian restaurant with your book club and try some of the foods that Tunde eats in the book. While there, discuss the importance of food in culture and identity. How does it bring people together? What does it represent? How can it tie in to one's own sense of self? Take this discussion a step further at your next book club meeting and bring a dish from your own childhood or culture that is particularly meaningful to you. Make sure to bring enough for everyone!

2. Music is one of the ways in which Tunde begins to explore and experiment with his identity. At your next book club meeting, listen to a few of the albums that Tunde may have listened to in the book: *Dangerous* by Michael Jackson, *II* by Boyz II Men, and *The Score* by the Fugees. Despite how different these artists are from one another, is there any common thread that runs through all three of them? Discuss how this can be used

as a metaphor for the complexity of identity. How can aspects of ourselves that are seemingly so different from one another come together to create one cohesive whole? How might one aspect of our identity come out in a stronger way than others at times? Reflect with your book club.

3. *A Particular Kind of Black Man* is framed as Tunde's attempt to record his memories when he becomes fearful he is losing his sense of reality. But memory is a tricky thing! Think of an experience that you had—either recently or while you were growing up—in which someone else was present. Write down that "story," being as meticulous as you can about the details. Then, ask the person who participated in that experience with you to also write down the story, being just as meticulous. Once both of your stories are written down, share and compare them. What is similar about your memories? Different? Share the findings with your book club. Why might we remember an event differently from someone else who shared in the experience with us? Is it possible for our memories to change over time?

4. Tunde moves around a lot, both as a child and as a young adult. Using a world map, mark all of the locations that Tunde lives in and visits in the book—from Utah to Texas to Maine to Nigeria—and look up some

of the tourist destinations in each city. Where would you visit were you to go on a "road trip" with Tunde? Why? Then, create your own map of all of the places that you've visited and lived, both in the United States and throughout the world. Do your best to remember as many places as you can, and share your maps with your book club. What's one spot you would take them all to visit if you could? If it's close by, plan a field trip!

5. Stay updated on Tope Folarin's latest projects. Visit Folarin's website, https://www.topefolarin.com, and follow him on Twitter (@topefolarin) and Facebook to learn about some of his other published works and to hear what he's working on next.